SECRETS BELOW THE WATER

They'll never be the same again...

SAMANTHA MOSS

CEDAR HILL PUBLISHING

Secrets Below the Water

Copyright © 2004 Samantha Moss   All Rights Reserved

Cover by Rebecca Hayes

Book design and editing by Rebecca Hayes

Published in the United States by
Cedar Hill Publishing
P.O. Box 905
Snowflake, Arizona 85937
http://www.cedarhillpublishing.com

Library of Congress Control Number
2004116706

ISBN 1-932373-93-4

Acknowledgements

*I wish to dedicate "Secrets Below The Water" to
Jim Terry for his support and believing in me. My close friends who shared this adventure. A special "Thanks" to Ross Wood for his guidance in making it a reality at long last.
With Love, Gratitude and Respect,
Samantha Moss*

INTRODUCTION

The mystical waters of Eagles Lake was part of the Tennessee River Valley's project for flood control for the Cumberland Plateau. The lake was hidden deep in the foothills of the Appalachian Mountains. The tragic secrets the lake held for so many years were now about to show themselves to the crew on board the houseboat, "The Stardust," for this was where the couples had chosen to escape their busy city lives for a week's vacation together.

The Lake with its captivating crystal blue waters was famous for house-boating as well as a fisherman's paradise. This spectacular place looked to meet all their expectations for a fun-filled dream vacation. Yet none of them knew the horrifying secrets the lake's amazing blue waters held, that were about to become their unbelievable nightmare.

Betty and David Stuart were one of the four couples. They lived a very busy lifestyle. David was a detective on the police force of his hometown, which in it's self was a very stressful and drama-filled profession. He lived with life and death situations every day. He knew when he left home for his job each day, he may not be able see his family again. There was always a chance he would be killed in the line of duty. David was involved in other community activities, as well, that he and his family enjoyed together.

Betty was just like her husband, busy. She was a registered nurse and worked at a major hospital. In the hospital she saw as much drama as her husband did. She helped with the people who sometimes had gotten hurt by the same people her husband had to deal with on a daily basis. With all this going on in their lives they hoped that their vacation each year would come sooner than it always did. They looked forward to spending at least this one-week away from the busy city life they lived and enjoy having a relaxing time with their friends.

Lilly and John Woods had lives different from the other three couples. Lilly was a Cherokee Indian, a very spiritual lady. Her bead work had made her famous. She was also the best seamstress in the area, well known for her beautiful beaded designs. Her work was sought by many of the wealthiest ladies in the state. Some of the fanciest suits and dresses ever made for women were handmade by Lilly in her own home. This required her to be home more than the other three women.

Her fascination on the other hand was with her own Indian culture and rituals. Many hours she studied the Native American medicines and had an incomparable herb garden she shared with her family and closest friends. For hundred of years the Native Americans had used these plants for healing of all kinds, and burned sacred plants to keep negative energies away and restore balance to their lives. Lilly believed in doing this on a regular basis to reduce her stress and keep harmony and balance in her and John's life.

John, her husband, was a carpenter and carver. He spent much of his time alone in his shop, where he worked long hours designing wooden statues. He turned out many fine carvings of animals, birds and some beautiful pieces of furniture. But his real enjoyment was the outdoors, hunting, fishing and even trapping.

John and Lilly both found this week with their close friends gave them an opportunity to be close to nature and also have other people to talk to for a change, other than with just each other.

Lilly had a real need to get away from her work for awhile because of the physical stress she had been feeling. Her beading was very hard on her eyes, hands and back. She needed rest from her work very badly. Plus her sleep had been invaded lately by nightmares.

Her nightmares were becoming a nightly occurrence. She was being tormented by the dreams or visions of a white spirit, drifting just above a pool of whirling dark water. Then hands reaching out for her, pulling and tugging, edging her down into the water's depth.

This dream was so real that when she woke in a panic, night after night her body would be drenched with sweat from fighting the demon within her nightmare. She was unable to deny she was indeed in need of a few peaceful nights of sleep. These visions had started from the moment she and the others had talked about their vacation trip for this year.

Was the Spirit world trying to reach out to her, or was her own mind playing games? she wondered. She prayed for spiritual guidance for relief from these nightmares. Maybe she was just tired and was causing these visions to herself.

Brenda and Don Roberts were just as excited about this week of vacationing with their close friends as the others were. Brenda was a dance instructor at a neighborhood fitness center. She lived for the vacations they all took together and her workouts at the center kept her in shape for the activities they enjoyed. Water sports and boating was her favorite things.

Brenda had always wanted to go on a cruise ship but hadn't been able to talk the others into it, so far. She enjoyed their vacations because of the places they chose to visit always had plenty sun and peaceful beaches, but was also filled with excitement. She would tell the others to "live on the edge," which she did herself.

Brenda had a drive to stay fit and enjoy life to the fullest as if there was no tomorrow. Having been diagnosed with rheumatoid arthritis at an early age she was bound and determined to enjoy her life while she could. She was like a kid with a new toy when it came to new adventures. Her excitement for enjoying life was what encouraged the others to do things out of the ordinary.

Her husband Don had been a musician since the age of 10. He was raised in the south with the love for country music as well as rock and roll. He had played for or with many of the top music performers. He made a nice living doing just what his heart loved most, making music and making people smile.

He had a serious side to him but not many saw it. He had been raised by his grandparents after losing his mother and father at an early age of two. He had gotten into trouble when he was a teen but over the years worked to be a better man. His anger was due to the loss of his parents but over time he knew how lucky he was to have loving grandparents. He enjoyed life as much as his wife.

Last of the four couples was Ann and Jim Perry. Jim was a government Aerospace Engineer, working for the Air Force, a very practical man who believed that there were always logical answers to every problem. You just had to look harder sometimes to find them. He had dreamed of becoming a fighter pilot but the closest he could come was having an eye and the scientific knowledge to design what he loved most.

He was color blind and this stopped his dream in its tracks. The next best thing was to be able to fly the smaller planes and he wasted no time in getting his license. His other hobby was motorcycles. It was the one thing he and Ann disagreed about. She was afraid he would get hurt or killed on one of his bikes. She didn't have a problem with him using his talent to build the cycles but just didn't want him to ride them.

Ann was an entrepreneur in every sense of the word. She and Jim owned three other businesses, one of which was her pride and joy. It was a stainless steel diner like the old fashion dining cars of the 1950's. Her son managed it for them..

She loved people and nature. The one thing she most enjoyed was fishing and boating. This was the tie between the four couples. They all loved boating and the outdoors. Ann was always willing to help anyone in need. She never judged anyone on first impressions. She was there for friends and others who needed her help in any way.

Lilly and Ann were Sisters of the same blood, both Cherokee. Both had fire in their heart for Mother Earth. This is what had brought them together as friends.

Being busy with their day to day life it was difficult for them to have the time to see and socialize with each other.

They set a date with the others for vacation of fun and excitement every year for the same time, the first week of July. This was the seventh year they had all spent their vacation together. By this time the four couples knew each other very well.

They had no idea that this vacation would bring them closer than they had ever been before.

DAY ONE

Eagles Lake was about the most beautiful place they had chosen to vacation in the past seven years. The lake was nestled in the Cumberland foothills. The Perry's had received some wonderful information on house-boating from one of the marina's on the lake called Star Point.

They thought that house-boating would be filled with new experiences that none of the other couples had experienced before. This would be a new exciting adventure for them all.

The lake greeted them with unsurpassed natural beauty. It also provided 30,000 acres of beautiful clear water, offering a wide variety of water sports and fishing. This was the perfect place for them to come to really enjoy themselves. There were many hidden coves and arms off the main body of the lake that could keep them for days without seeing another human, if they preferred.

They arrived at the marina to pick up their houseboat at about two in the afternoon on Sunday, July 1, a beautifully sunny warm day. All of them had been in agreement as to what each one's responsibility on this trip would be ahead of time. So the next step was for Jim and Don to received instructions on how to operate the large 54' houseboat. The others looked on as the man showed them how to maneuver through the waterways of the lake. They received very detailed instructions on how to anchor or tie up the boat so the wind or maybe a storm wouldn't cause them to be in danger.

After the instructions, they were ready to ease the houseboat out of the channel and be on their way to find the perfect cove, where they would spend their first relaxing night

While the guys were at the marina, getting bait and checking out the batteries and other supplies, the women went in search of someone who could give them directions to a marina with a restaurant and gift shop.

The cashier at the boat dock told them there were so many places to shop and enjoy good food, but that they needed a map if this was their first time to Eagles Lake. She told them that there were a total of 14 marinas around the lake at this time. They were also informed that there were no private boat docks anywhere on the lake itself.

She went to check and see if they still had maps in the backroom. She returned shortly with a map, but she informed them that this one was old and very much out of date as far as the new marinas were concerned. This map did show the lake, however, and how it was laid out when it was built about seventy year ago. Back in 1932-33. They all laughed and thanked the woman for all her help. Ann was glad to get a map of any kind showing the lake and the fingers off the main body of water. They could at least find where they were in case they got split up and lost from the houseboat. Now they were off to meet up with the guys.

Meanwhile David and John had taken the runabouts, which belonged to David and Jim, and launched them. They could tie them to the sides of the houseboat and cruise until after they found a cove to tie up in for the night. They had traveled for about one hour when they came to a fork in the lake. It had a finger that lead back into secluded area that off the main lake and was perfect for the night.

It was a lovely cove with lush green forest on three sides, totally isolated. It took them two hours to put away their supplies of groceries, set up beds, and put the linens and clothes away.

The men readied their fishing gear, and checked the boats to make sure the batteries were charged and ready for their next few days of fun in the sun. As night approached they decided to have the girls make ham and cheese sandwiches instead of preparing a large meal, and retire to bed early this evening so they would be feeling great for the next day. The long drive had made them all a little weary.

At about thirty minutes after midnight the waters of their cove began to rock the houseboat, as if it was a cradle being rocked side to side gently. The movement woke Lilly and Ann. They laid in the dark and listened for the noises outside. There weren't any to be heard. It was dead silent, so they soon drifted off to sleep again.

A short time later, Don and David were the next ones to be awakened by the rocking, which had grown much stronger this time. Don decided to get up and check out the runabouts, making sure they were tied up securely. He noticed that the rocking had stopped. It must have been a boat passing the entrance of their cove that made the heavy rocking that woke them up, he thought.

How calm and lovely the water was at this time of morning when mists rose along the surface of the water, next to the shore. But the moon was high in the sky and this gave a pale light to the shoreline. He noticed that the water about eight feet away from the Stardust looked just like someone had turned on an underwater light ,from deep down below the surface.

Don thought at first it was from the moonlight but when looking closer he noticed that the area was dark around this light. It was just in one section of the cove. The center. As a matter of fact the light seemed to be moving slowly in the direction of the boat and him. He grinned, shook his head and decided to go back to bed before his imagination ran wild. As he entered the door of the Stardust he turned to give a quick glance to the spot where the light had been. He saw nothing but the calm water.

David asked Don if everything was okay. "Yes, I just checked everything," Don said as he settled again into his bunk. They both went back to sleep.

Secrets Below the Water

DAY TWO

Morning greeted them around 6:00 AM with the sunrise. Lilly had made coffee and was enjoying her first cup on the front sun deck of the Stardust.

When Lilly was at home, she always enjoyed her first cup of coffee on their patio. Which looked out onto her garden. Lilly was the kind of woman that paid much respect to nature with all its remarkable beauty. Raised in the West, she learned early in life to appreciate wildlife and all Mother Earth had to offer. She was oval faced, with coal black hair and perfect olive skin. Her eyes were like wild black diamonds and at this moment they glistened with excitement as she looked out over the bow of the boat.

She called as softly as she could to the others to come look; there were about four white-tailed deer approximately fifteen feet away. They had just wandered down to the water's edge for an early morning drink. Everyone came out to have a look, but the movement on the houseboat made by all of them at once was felt by the deer, which headed back into the forest.

"This is exactly where I always dreamed of being," John said. "Things smell so fresh and clean."

After their first morning's breakfast together and the galley was cleaned up, they decided to go for a boat ride around the lake to check out some of the sites and activities at one or two of the marinas, so they could participate in them later. Jim was getting impatient to be in the water, and couldn't wait for them to decide where they were going first.

He asked if they would hook up the tube to the boat, he wanted to go tubing. They pulled him along behind the boat. Ann loved to watch her husband. He was tall, broad shouldered, with an aura of power and authority. His features added up to handsome. A strong face with a high and wide forehead, covered with dark wavy auburn hair. A smooth bronze complexion accentuated his high cheekbones. His mouth was full and sensuous. But his eyes were what she always found most attractive. They were clear bright emerald green, large and wide, like a cat's eyes.

He is gorgeous, she thought, watching the water sparkle on his skin as he enjoyed riding the tube. Jim loved to be in the water and this was beautifully clear water. Most of the lakes around Ohio (where they were from) were either to dirty or too shallow to enjoy the way he was enjoying this ride. The water felt so cool and refreshing to his skin.

Ann got out the map she had received at the marina so they could look over the area and decide where they wanted to go first. They headed for the west end of the lake about ten miles by boat from their little cove and the Stardust.

There were three nice size islands out on Eagles Lake. They passed Goats Island, Pine Island and were approaching Divers Island. Just as they were going by Pine Island, Lilly got a chill and felt as if she had been there before. She quickly put it out of her mind. She had slept all night without waking up with the nightmares she had been experiencing at home for the past few months. So nothing was going to change the wonderful mood she was in today.

David said, "It really amazes me how an island like Divers Island came about." It was almost totally a rock formation that rose up out of the water with a single oak tree that looked to be at least two hundred years old, in the center of the island. This was at a very deep part of the lake. The depth of the lake at this point was about one hundred fifty feet. The island was about one hundred twenty feet out in the lake from the edge to the main shoreline.

Someone had told David that when the lake was formed they sank an old fishing boat so it would bring in divers to the area and make money for the marina owners. At any marina on Eagles Lake you could rent diving equipment and if you had never gone diving, you could receive lessons. There were six other spots for divers to enjoy, but this area was popular and David wanted to investigate it for himself. Don was interested in the old boat and how they had chosen this area to sink it. Don and David told the others they would check it out later.

"Lets go have lunch," said Jim.

After lunch they headed back to the Stardust. It was late afternoon and they all decided to relax. The girls couldn't wait to hit the water and cool off. The temperature was about ninety-seven degrees. They let the guys take their naps while they cooled off in the cove. Ann was the first to enter the water.

After about ten minutes, Betty heard a splash a little to her left. She asked, "Did you all hear that?" Lilly laughingly said, "It's probably a trout jumping at a moth or a fly." For some reason Betty felt strange, and a little afraid. She wasn't quite sure why she felt this way. The girls were having a ball splashing and swimming, but Betty was still conscious of this uncomfortable feeling she had.

She reasoned with herself that it was because she hadn't been in this much water in a year and this was her fear. Just knowing the depth of the water scared her a little. She didn't inform the other girls of her feelings because they were having such a great time.

They had been in the water for about an hour when Lilly felt like something was pushing up next to her legs. There weren't any weeds at the place where she was and the water was so clear, she could look down into the water and see her feet. Yet she had the strangest feeling that something was lightly pulling her with the slightest touch downward in the water.

Almost in a panic now, she remembered her dreams. She swam over to where Ann,

Brenda and Betty were. Still she felt as if it was touching her legs. She wanted to kick but knew nothing was there.

What was happening to her? She brushed it off. They were laughing and having a ball when right in the center of the four of them, a fish broke the surface of the water. They all laughed and the tension broke.

It was time to go in and get ready for their early dinner at one of the restaurants at the marina, so that they could cruise back after dinner and watch the sunset on the lake. They would need to be back at their cove before the sun had gone totally down.

Eagles Lake was too big and too dangerous to be caught out after dark, if you weren't very familiar with the area. Even then you had to be very cautious.

They had all agreed to have the Steak and Shrimp Special at the restaurant, which was wonderful. It was a spectacular sunset they witnessed on their cruise back to the cove. Just what they expected only more breathtaking.

As the couples headed into the cove where the houseboat was docked, they felt a sudden coldness , a change from the rest of the lake. The coldness was felt by all of them. Jim remarked that this area must be so shaded that it was cooler than the main lake this time of evening.

They tied the runabout to the Stardust and went inside. Brenda spoke first and said, "It feels like someone was here before us!" They looked but nothing was missing or even out of place. There was just this strange feeling all of them had, that someone had been in the houseboat while they were gone. No one said anymore about it. Brenda, Betty, Ann and Jim decided to play cards while Lilly, John, David and Don fished.

David and John sat talking and David mentioned to John that one of them needed to lock the houseboat up the next time they all left to go boating. He was certain that someone had been in the houseboat while they were out .Lilly was listening to the men talk but not wanting to let them know she heard them. John agreed with David and he knew David was a little concerned.

"John says that night is one of the best times to fish", Lilly informed them.

John spoke up and added, "Yeah, my Dad came from the old country and always told us the best time to fish was between dusk and midnight."

"What do you mean by the old country?" asked Don.

"Greece", says John.

David watched the others fish, even through fishing was why he had wanted to come to Eagles Lake so much. He was enjoying the peaceful and beautiful view he saw as he looked out over the water. Even through it was well into the evening, David noticed the sky was still the most vivid blue he had seen anywhere. Once again he thought, "this is Paradise. This is what I had hoped to come here and find."

Don was also aware of the evening, it was as beautiful as the evening before. After about three hours a cloud covered the moon, for a short time making everyone aware of the sudden enveloping darkness. Don watched the moon come back up on the lake. He remarked to David and the others about how the waters glistened in the moonlight. David agreed that it was outstanding to look at. The others decided to head in for bed at around half passed eleven, but Don decided to try his luck a little longer. When everyone had been gone for approximately 30 minutes or so, he noticed the silence. The air was still and warm. Don noticed that not a breath of air was stirring at that moment, the waves were silent and the trees weren't moving. Everything was deadly still.

There was only a silvery gray fog moving in on the cove, but it was coming in very fast. The fog just covered a narrow path. It didn't cover the whole cove in front of him like he would have expected it to. Almost as if the moon was shinning through it.

That was it; there was a light shining through the fog. That was what he saw the other night. He laughed to himself, but as he looked at the fog now, he wasn't sure why, but it still looked so ominous to him. There was a swirling noise in the water where the fog looked to be the thickest.

Curious, Don eased toward the back railing of the boat, stepping carefully to avoid making a sound that might frighten away whatever it was. He did glance over his left shoulder to the bank. The moonlight slanting between the trees turned the water to silver as it rushed between the bank and the houseboat. He saw nothing, but when he looked back at the fog it was upon the boat and him by this time and the noise was much louder.

There was wind that came out of nowhere that was so strong that it pushed him back, back against the back wall of the boat and something was holding him there as if it was a powerful force of hands. He knew no one was with him. He tried to move but found he could not. By this time Don became aware of the pounding of his heart as if it was trying to escape out of his body. It was now getting harder to breathe.

It was as if someone was holding him there with hands around his neck. But there was no one there. It was the fog that had him trapped. Suddenly water splashed in thousands of droplets as a figure broke through the surface. This was so unreal that Don found himself wondering if what he saw and felt was really happening.

Through all this he could not utter a sound or move an inch. The figure moved toward him. It was the figure of a man, but Don knew what he saw wasn't a human… it was a GHOST. He was spellbound and wondered if maybe he was hallucinating. While he watched the vision of a man take form in front of him, he felt the power of the energy surrounding it. A moment later Brenda called to Don, to come in for the night.

As Brenda spoke it seem to change the power of the figure in front of him. He felt a strange sensation as the fog and ghost, if that's what it was, dissipated back into the water. He could breathe again. The trees were moving and the air was fresh again. There was a very bright light within the fog just like the light he saw the night before. In a moment it was gone.

He stood there a little shaken, not believing what had really happened to him. Brenda called to Don again to come to bed. He called back to her, "I'll be there in a little while." Don knew that he couldn't let the others know what had taken place. As a matter of fact, he wasn't sure himself.

For another brief moment he stood looking out over the water trying to make some sense out of what had taken place. The ghostly figure had the most haunting eyes he could ever imagine. For an eerie moment Don thought to himself that he had looked into the eyes of the devil. He managed to pull himself together before he went inside to Brenda and went in to bed.

As he entered the boat, Brenda said, "I thought you were never coming in, Don." He asked her if she had heard anything a few minutes ago.

She replied that she had been lying there daydreaming. "I could have dosed off for awhile I guess, Why?"

"Oh, I just wondered that's all." Don leaned over and gave Brenda a kiss good night. After about an hour he started to fall asleep himself.

Secrets Below the Water

DAY THREE

The crew on board the Stardust awoke to another bright sunny morning. After breakfast they were ready for some more exploring, everyone loaded up into the runabouts. Don wanted to have the houseboat moved to another cove, but was voted down by the others. They liked this cove because of the seclusion and wanted to remain here for at least one more night.

Betty said, "Let's look for another cove while we are out today. I know we can find one just as nice or better than this one. After all, we can move as much as we want, a different cove everyday. We could live like a band of gypsies for this week. Always on the move, a different cove every night."

Laughing at that remark, everyone agreed that they would look for a new cove and move early in the morning. Don was glad about the upcoming move. He didn't really want to spend another night in this cove. He might have had to tell the others about the experience he had the night before.

They loaded into the two runabouts and were off for some sun and fun, skiing and tubing. Jim was on the tube before they left the cove.

Brenda and Betty wanted to do some skiing as soon as they were on the main part of the lake. Brenda was a wonderful skier and could stay up about as long as Jim could be pulled on the tube.

After about an hour of skiing and tubing they decided to pull over closer to the shoreline so the rest of the crew could do some swimming. Mostly just horsing around, that is. This cooled them off. The day was growing warmer by the moment. By noontime they decided to put up the tops on the boats and go exploring to find another cove.

The lake had so many coves that a person could get lost for quiet a long time. They passed Divers Island and headed up to the

North of it, to the Black Hawk Marina. David couldn't take his eyes off the island. He told the others that he wanted to check this island out before long. Lilly also liked the island and would enjoy walking around looking at things or just sitting under the big oak tree.

Jim said they would stop there on their way back from lunch if they wanted. "Great," said David.

Lunch at the Marina was what they needed to feel ready to continue their exploring of Eagles Lake. They checked out all the coves they came to on the way back to Divers Island. There was a cove just a short distance away from Divers Island that was perfect for a night's stay. They could spend time on the island while anchored in the cove. So this was the plan of action for the next morning, to move closer to Divers Island.

It was four in the afternoon when the two runabouts entered the cove and everyone gazed upon the Stardust. As before they were tried and wanted to rest awhile. Lilly decided to relax by reading the book she had brought with her. The others did whatever they wanted to relax. This gave them freedom from each other for a while. Everyone could have time to themselves.

Jim and David decided to take a nap. Betty fixed herself and John a tall glass of ice tea, which they had on the front sun deck of the Stardust.

"This is as pleasant as anyone could ask for," John remarked. Betty agreed that being out with nature was as uplifting as anything she had ever done. Brenda, Ann and Don played cards.

Lilly was reading her book on Indian customs and spirits when she suddenly felt as if someone was with her in the galley of the houseboat. She looked up from the book to make sure someone hadn't come in from outside. There was not a soul there, but the feeling was still strong as if there was someone with her.

Without realizing what she was doing, she reached out her hand in front of her as if to touch something. She felt coldness, the same as the other day in the lake, as if she had laid her hand on ice. She drew her hand back quickly and closed the book. When she looked up again, she was startled, a faint vision of a young man was taking form in front of her.

Lilly sat perfectly still for an instant and then rose from her chair. The vision was still there, only now it was as if the young man was trying to tell her something. He looked so sad as if he was almost weeping. She moved to the center of the room to where he was and put out her hand to touch him. She knew this was a spirit not a person. As she did this he backed up and she felt the extreme coldness in the room.

Lilly tried to speak, but at that second, he disappeared from view. "Wait!" she called after him, but it was too late. Lilly wanted desperately to find an answer to this, and at the same time she couldn't bring herself to believe what had happen. Maybe she was tired and had read to long. After all, she had been reading about Indian spirits returning to help out their tribe. This was too much for her to absorb. She wondered if the visions she had been having at home were part of this. Was she ill or losing her mind?

She looked out on the front of the houseboat to where Betty and John were. She decided to join them in a glass of tea. Desperately Lilly wanted to tell John and Betty about the vision but decided now wasn't the time. She would wait. She could have been tired from reading and thought she saw this spirit. Forget it, she told herself. Forget it before they think your crazy.

Ann remarked to Jim and Brenda, "This is turning out to be a wonderful vacation place."

She loved being away from the city and that busy life-style.

Brenda said, "This place has so much beauty that anyone would enjoy themselves." Jim agreed with the girls. Only he wondered if maybe people who live along the coast near the ocean enjoyed longer, happier lives than he and Ann would, living in Ohio. He made a promise to himself that he would check it out when they returned home to Ohio. He would love to live close to water. He knew that Ann would like that also.

Tonight was John's night to cook for the crew, while he prepared the grill for the steaks and Lilly made the salad. Don and Brenda decided to go explore the shoreline in front of the boat.

David said, "Don't get lost, and come back in an hour, because dinner should be ready by then. Also you two had better keep an eye out for snakes. The man at the marina warned us of snakes being around the rocky ledges and woodpiles or in tall grass. They don't have rattlers around here, but the black snakes and copperheads are everywhere."

Don said "Okay," took Brenda's hand to help her off the Stardust.

About 100 yards away from the boat they noticed a small pool of water and decided to take a look. Brenda found a fallen tree extending part way across the water. She climbed onto it and leaped to the other side of the water. Don was just coming up to the tree. "Come on, babe," she called to him.

Brenda bent down to look into the water. As she studied the water more closely she saw a face staring back up at her. She jumped up and screamed. Don was crossing over the tree at that point and asked, "What's wrong?" Brenda stood there with her hands over her mouth, looking at the water.

"There's a man's face in the water", Brenda said. Don went to the edge of the water to take a look for himself.

"Nothing is here, Brenda, you must have seen your face with a shadow across it or something", Don laughed. Thinking to himself how strange she would say she saw a man's face. Thinking about the night before and the evil face he had seen at came from the water.

Brenda said, "NO, Don, it was a man's face staring up at me." Don searched the pool of water but no sign of anyone. He put his arm around Brenda to comfort her.

"It's getting dark and we had better be heading back for dinner or John will send one of the others to come find us. Dinner has to be ready by now," he suggested.

Brenda was still shaken up by the incident. She knew she had seen a man's face. She felt sure she could describe him. Don held his arm around her and they walked slowly back. As they came with the sight of the boat he took her in his arms and held her close. "Lady, you know I love you don't you?" he asked her. She just shook her head and reach up to his face, planting kisses all over his face and neck. Don said, "Hey, better stop that right now or you're in big trouble." Laughing at that, they moved on down the path hand in hand.

As they reached the houseboat, John called out that dinner was being served. Everyone was in such a great mood. They were so different in their careers and life-styles but went together perfectly. They really enjoyed each other's company. Betty told John that they would let him cook anytime he wanted.

Dinner was superb. They all noticed the lovely evening sky. As the sunset, the horizon became layered with colors, lavenders and pale violets and amazing blues.

After all the dishes were done the girls had a surprise for the guys. They had always played little jokes on their men and this vacation wasn't going to be any different. They had picked up squirt guns at the Black Hawk Marina that very afternoon and now they were going to have fun. They loaded the guns with water. Betty said them they had better change back into their swimsuits because they definitely were going to get wet.

Now they were ready to get their revenge on the guys. Laughing they went out to where the men were on the back end of the boat. As they approached they pulled out their guns and told the guys to stand up or they would shoot. David laughed. This was right up his alley.

"Oh, really", said Jim as they opened fire. The guys started for the guns as the girls ran. Ann jumped into the water first. The others joined her soon. Jim grabbed Ann's arm and pulled her down under the water where he gave her a big kiss. Brenda was the only one not in the water. She hid inside the closet in the galley.

Don went looking for her but found David's pail he used for bait. He filled it with water and went up on top of the boat to wait till Brenda came out the back door. He knew she would come out of hiding soon. Then he would pour the water on her as she walked through the door.

As Don had suspected Brenda was getting impatient and decided to go look for him and the others. As she came out of the closet there in front of her was the face she had seen in the pool of water earlier. He was just staring at her, but he was pale white and she could see through him. "God, am I seeing a ghost?" she thought to herself. The face moved in her direction slowly, then seemed to move back as if not really wanting a confrontation with her either.

She was frightened; she looked at him once more and ran for the back door. As soon as she opened the door, Don poured the pail of water over her head. Brenda was almost hysterical by this time and started to cry.

Don was down to her instantly. "Babe, I'm sorry, I thought you wanted to have fun not get upset." He put his arms around her and sat her in a chair. The others stopped horsing around and watched what was happening on the boat with Brenda and Don. Ann called out to Don, "Is everything okay up there?"

Don answered that Brenda was just shaken up by the water being poured on her like he did. "Well, its getting cool in the water so we will all come in and join the two of you", Ann called back to Don.

Uneasiness had settled over Brenda, as she sat in a chair on the rear of the houseboat and looked out onto the lake. The moonlight was calming most of the time, but not tonight.

The others on board were enjoying the sounds of the night. The frogs croaking even bothered her.

Obeying an impulse, she stared into the shadows of the night and shouted, "I saw you! No one answered, not even the frogs. Don reached out to touch her and the others asked what was going on. Don told them what had happened when they went for their walk and that he hadn't seen anyone. He was sure she had seen something, only he didn't want to admit it.

"Brenda, was it a young man's face you saw?" asked Lilly. Don asked Lilly not to encourage her. "I have my reasons", said Lilly. Don really wanted to tell what had been happening to him but thought better of it. Brenda looked at them all before she answered.

"Lilly, I saw a man's face, and I guess you could say he wasn't old."

Jim laughed and remarked that we all should try sitting around in the dark telling ghost stories. Brenda replied that when she hid from Don in the galley, she saw the face again. Only this time it wasn't just the face she saw, it was the whole person, except the face was what she noticed most. When she opened the door of the closet to come out, he was standing there. "Lilly, he's a ghost, I know it because I could see right through his body".

"I believe her", Lilly said. "I have read about spirits returning." Most of the time they are still earth bound because of the way they left this world."

"I think what we all need is to move out of this cove first thing in the morning", Don said. They all looked around at each other in agreement. They went to bed that night earlier than usual. Each one had their own thoughts on what Brenda had seen and what Lilly had said about spirits, but no one wanted to talk about it.

Around half passed midnight Don was awakened by coldness in the room. He reached for the blanket at the end of the bed, but stopped quickly. At the end of the bed was the hazy figure of a person. A man. He sat up in bed and for moment stared at the faint figure. He was waiting for something awful to happen like the other night. The vision started to move coming past him, he noticed a very musky dirt smell filled the air. The ghost moved slowly down to the end of the hallway. Don got out of bed to follow.

As the figure moved into the galley, Don lost sight of it for a moment. When he entered the galley, he saw that the figure was more vivid. He knew that it had to be the young man Brenda had seen. The ghost picked up the book that Lilly had been reading and left on the table.

He turned the pages and stopped on one, laid the book down with the pages open and moved in Don's direction again. It was as if he didn't even see Don at this point. His eyes never looked at Don but straight ahead, back down the hallway.

As he passed Don, the room became icy cold. Don turned to follow but again the vision had disappeared. The room was no longer cold.

Don knew for certain the very moment, the very instant, that the ghost had laid down the book that he, Don, was supposed to read it. He walked over to the book that lay open on the table. He read the pages but it had no meaning to him. So Don laid the book down with the pages still open. In the morning he would pick it up and read it again. He knew he must tell the others what had happened. He wanted to wake Lilly but thought better of it.

What's going on, he wondered, *I don't believe in ghosts!* But what he had witnessed he knew something was definitely wrong. He went back to bed and did fall off to sleep even through he didn't think he would ever sleep again. He knew he must convince the crew to move from this area as soon as the sun came up on the horizon.

DAY FOUR

The next morning everyone had breakfast together while Don told them what happened to him during the night. He went over to the table and picked up the book. Don asked, "Lilly, would you read these two pages and see what you get out of them? I read them last night after he disappeared. But nothing jumped out at me." Jim laughed when Don said nothing jumped out at him.

"I know he is trying to tell us something," said Brenda.

"I don't feel he is going to do us harm. Do you Don?" Lilly asked.

"Well, to be very truthful about the whole thing, Yes, Yes I do."

At that point Don told them about the first night he had seen the ghost. That he was certain that he would have killed him if Brenda had not called out to him to come in to bed.

Jim just shook his head and went on with his breakfast. David and Betty really didn't believe what seemed to be taking place. But David was a detective, and he would wait to see what the facts were and then let the others know what he thought was going on with this cove and the visions. Jim and David both knew there had to be a logical reasoning to this madness.

Betty couldn't bring herself to believe in ghosts, though she had heard talk from other nurses at the hospital about seeing a ghost in the room of a patient that was on the critically ill list or that was dying. This was different; no one here was in a critical state.

Ann sat and listened to what Don was telling them, that he had seem this spirit on at least two other occasions by this time.

She felt the ghost would have done harm by now if he had wanted to, so maybe he was trying to communicate with them.

Jim was a realist. Things can always be explained. He felt this was no different, that there was a logical answer. Jim just didn't believe in the supernatural. Ann was a very superstitious person, but at the same time she didn't really believe in visions, or ghosts, as some people might think a person who is superstitious would believe. She believed in the Spirit world because of the other stories the Cherokee Storytellers told, but not like these things that were happening to her friends right here right now.

But then they both knew something was happening to their friends. Jim waited till Don had finished and then asked, "Don't you think that maybe we can explain the visions? After all you have only seen him at night and the fog or mist around here is quite thick at times and can play tricks on your eyes."

David and the others, except for Lilly and Brenda, laughed and agreed that had to be the cause for Don and Brenda's mysterious person. After all, most of the others hadn't seen it. Jim asked, "Why do you think it has singled out you and Brenda?"

Don said, "I really don't know, but I have seen a ghost!"

Lilly kept silent and waited to see Don's reaction to the answer that Jim gave. She was not asked by anyone of them why she had inquired as to the age of the man's face Brenda had seen in the water the night before. She didn't know if she should reveal what had taken place in the galley the other afternoon. But, one thing was for sure; there was a ghost or spirit in that cove with them. All she could think of was, *why is he there!*

From the things she had read on spirits, there was a reason and that the spirit would sooner or later let them know if they stayed there. Don looked at Jim and said, "I really do believe I saw a ghost and that he is trying to communicate with me. I also believe he could do harm to any one of us if he wanted to."

Jim just shook his head grinning and said; "I think we had better move this here houseboat to another cove now before we all start hallucinating."

Lilly decided to keep quiet for now. They started to tie down everything on board the Stardust so they could pull the boat out of the cove and be on the move in a short time.

John made sure the fishing equipment was fixed so it wouldn't get blown overboard into the water. David and Jim jumped into the runabouts and moved out away from the houseboat as John backed the large boat out of the cove. It was too large of a boat to just back a little ways out and turn. Much too close quarters for that.

The girls did the dishes and enjoyed the ride to the cove they had picked out the day before, near Divers Island. Everyone was in good spirits. Lilly wondered if this would end whatever had been going on with them. She looked over at Don. By his expression, he was glad to be moving away from the cove. Don glanced in Lilly's direction and they studied each other but not a word was spoken.

Lilly remembered that Don had asked her to look at the book. With all the commotion she had not picked up the book at all. She got up and walked over to the table where the book was and started to read the two pages Don had ask her to. The pages talked about Indian burials and that was it. Nothing made her think of ghosts or visions of young men. Before she put the book down she marked the pages. Maybe later she would pick out something that might have meaning. Don watched Lilly but said nothing to her. She did look in his direction when she had finished the two pages and shook her head at Don, to let him know nothing meant anything to her in reference to the vision.

The Stardust rounded the bend near Divers Island and the crew noticed the view of the main part of the lake was spectacular today. There was no breeze and the temperature was high in the nineties. They pulled into the cove near Diver's Island and tied up. They were just finishing when Jim and David came up along side of the houseboat to tie up the runabouts.

This cove wasn't as secluded as the one they had just left. Here they tied up to the banks instead of anchoring in the cove.

"We could have a bonfire and roast marshmallows tonight," Betty said. "A fire would keep the bad spirits away," she said to John and they both laughed and got back on board the boat, after making sure they were tied up securely.

This move had taken about three hours. Ann remarked, "This is a great place to have lunch with friends." She was getting hungry by this time, so were the others?

David could hardly eat for thinking of Divers Island. The back of the boat where they had lunch had a view of the island and it was very difficult to get David to think of anything but that. He ate part of the sandwich and jumped up and said, "Lets get going we're wasting good daylight. I want to see what is on the island."

All of them decided to go except for Ann. She was not up to doing anything, really. She told them to go ahead and she would prepare the baked beans and salad for dinner tonight. They took both of the runabouts and headed off for the Island.

Ann decided to just relax and sun bathe. She could see them from the top of the houseboat. After about an hour she went in to take a shower and freshen up before they returned. She put the beans in the oven and started the salad when she noticed that the room was filled with the scent of orange blossoms. She knew that orange groves didn't grow in the middle of Tennessee. She was almost overpowered by the fragrance.

She went to the front of the boat and looked around to make sure there weren't any orange trees. She laughed at herself for doing that. Something in the galley had to be related to the scent. She went back to slicing the tomatoes and onions.

Meanwhile the others were having a great time on Divers Island. Lilly and Betty had come across a place where some other people had made a fire pit and now it was overtaken by little black and white butterflies. They were everywhere. David had found a place on the north side of the island that had a large hole going straight down into the bottom of the lake. How could this have been formed, he wondered. It was large enough for at least three people to swim in.

Jim told David he would dive down as far as he could and see what was there and if the hole did extend down into the lake. Betty dove down as far as she could. The water felt cool, but not cold to her skin. Jim dove in right after her. The hole looked like it had formed over the years by the water's power eroding the rock and not by man.

When they came up for air David said, "I'm going to rent some diving equipment and go down in the morning." David and Betty had diving experience and loved to find neat places to dive.

Jim wasn't a diver and said, "You can go and I'll be waiting right here for you, because it's way too deep for me."

Lilly had joined them by this time and all decided to head back for the houseboat till in the morning. "This island is interesting and full of surprises", Lilly said.

Back at the houseboat, Ann had finished the salad and baked beans and laid down for a quick nap. She awoke as the runabouts entered the cove. She asked, "Well, did you guys have fun exploring your island?"

They all said yes. Lilly told Ann about the butterflies and the hole on the north side of the island. Brenda helped Ann with dinner that evening. After dinner Betty and John built a fire on the shore in front of the Stardust. The fire felt really good because the air was cooler and there looked to be a storm approaching from the west.

After about an hour the storm was almost upon them. David was glad that they had tied the houseboat to the banks instead of being anchored in the cove. This way the boat was more secure. The weather was changing for the worse.

Off in the near distance thunder rumbled and the lightning danced all around the sky. The storm was now upon them and the lightning was coming closer. David joined the others on the back deck of the boat. It was covered by an awning, like on their patio at home.

From here they could watch the storm approaching and not get wet. The air was really cool by now and the rain was coming down hard, lightning hit a tree on the bank in front of the boat. There was a large thud from the falling tree. The fog was so thick that you couldn't see ten feet in front of you.

They decided to call it a night and go inside. As they entered the galley there was that scent of orange blossoms again.

Jim said, "Gee, doesn't it smell good in here?"

Betty asked, "Where is that smell coming from?"

"I don't know but it was over powering earlier this afternoon," said Ann.

"Did we bring oranges with us?" asked Don. "If so, I would like one."

The girls looked in the cabinets and closets but didn't find oranges. By this time the smell was gone. They fixed a snack of cookies and coffee or milk for the guys and went to prepare for bed. It was still raining and the rain on the roof was comforting. This caused all of them to fall to sleep in record time.

Sometime in the wee hours of the morning, Ann awoke and lay there listening to the sounds of the night and the rain, which had tapered off to a drizzle. She lay there and in the distance she thought she heard a woman crying. After a while she decided to get up and check out the galley and get a drink of water.

As she reached for a glass she stopped. There was the faint fragrance of orange blossoms, again. She filled the glass with water and walked out on the bow of the boat. Everything was quiet and peaceful, no orange blossoms in the air. The freshness of the outside was delightful to her. She took a towel and dried off one of the chairs to sit down in.

After enjoying the cool breeze for a while, she noticed that a misty fog was upon the front of the boat. She was startled to hear the sound of a woman weeping. As she looked deeper into the mist, it started to clear and a vision of a woman took form in front of her, in the very next chair.

She was a beautiful young woman in a high-necked lace dress. She had her hair up and a ribbon tied in it to match the dress she wore. Her face was warm and sweet looking with rosy coloring around her cheeks. The woman didn't even look in Ann's direction. She sat looking ahead of her as if not seeing Ann at all. She was weeping softly. Ann didn't move or even breathe for fear of scaring her away. She was fascinated by this lovely young woman that she knew was of another world, another time.

She sat spellbound and watched the vision with interest. The young woman began to weep harder and Ann saw she was holding something in her hand. As Ann looked closer at the woman she noticed it was a locket she wore around her neck. *I can't stand this*, Ann thought and decided to get up out of her chair and approach the woman.

The vision moved as Ann moved and in a second was gone. But Ann was over powered by the scent of orange blossoms.

So, she thought, *this is your scent. You have been in our presence when we smelled the fragrant of the orange blossoms. I just had my first encounter with a ghost,* she thought, a little frightened. This place must be filled with them.

She couldn't wait till daybreak to inform the others what had happened. While this was going on with Ann and the woman, Lilly had been awakened and heard the weeping. She had gotten out of bed and went to the galley. When she saw Ann on the bow of the boat she decided to join her but noticed that she wasn't alone. She too had seen the vision of the lovely young woman, but had decided to stay in the galley and watch.

Ann entered the galley and saw Lilly standing there. At first she was scared and jumped at the sight of Lilly standing there. Ann didn't expect to see her. Lilly was wearing a long white gown and in the darkness, she looked like a ghost herself. Ann said, "Shit, Lilly, you scared me." As she said that to Lilly, she knew that Lilly must have seen the vision of the woman also. "Lilly, did you see the woman on the front deck with me?" Ann spoke before Lilly could answer, "Please say yes!"

"Relax Ann, I did see the spirit of a young woman."

Ann felt better hearing this. "We must wake the others and tell them."

"No, not yet Ann. Lets wait till we make sure what the weeping woman is trying to tell us."

"What do you mean?" asked Ann.

"Well, we have had two different spirits, first the young man and now the weeping woman. There has to be a connection between the two of them, but what?"

Ann remarked, "The woman seems to be of another century because of the clothes she was wearing. Don't you think Lilly?"

"All I know is that we must find out why they are showing themselves to us. Lets wait till we see her again before we say anything to the others.

Secrets Below the Water

DAY FIVE

Sunrise brought them the smell of nice clean air. They had breakfast and while the girls did the dishes, the guys went for the diving equipment at the marina. David got himself and Betty the air tanks and all the equipment they needed to enjoy the day exploring Divers Island and told the man he would have it back by evening. They returned to the houseboat to pick up the others and head for Divers Island.

Ann wanted to stay on board the Stardust in hopes of seeing the ghost of the young woman again. Lilly told her all of them should go because it would be awhile before they made it back. Finally, Ann agreed to go.

Jim knew Ann loved to go out in the runabouts and explore, so why did she want to stay here anyway? This was a puzzle to him. He was glad when she agreed to go along with them.

They arrived at the island and it didn't take David and Betty long to suit up. They were ready to dive down the hole when Lilly told Betty to be careful. "As always" she said. The others watched as David and Betty descended into the water.

The water was easy to see in because it was crystal clear. David was already on the bottom by the time Betty reached it. They moved together slowly, along the bottom floor. Suddenly Betty saw what looked like a large oval stone lying on the bottom, just a short distance away from them. She motioned David to follow her, and he did.

There on the bottom was what appeared to be an old headstone. She wiped off the sediment with her hand and David tried to lift it, but it was too heavy. Betty cleaned off the stone, which by now they knew was a headstone from a grave, and David tried the flashlight, putting the beam on the stone so Betty could read the name. "Rebecca Jean Collins, Born 1889, Died 1920, Beloved Wife of Joshua.

She was only thirty-one years old when she died, Betty thought. They looked around the area but there wasn't anything else. Betty motioned David to go up top with her. They had to tell the others what they had found. David nodded his head in agreement and up they went.

The others waited impatiently for their return. Betty hit the surface first with David right behind her. Brenda yelled, "Yea!" and clapped her hands. "It's about time you came back to us", she said.

"You won't believe what we found down there," said Betty. "You just won't believe it." "What, tell us what you found," Jim demanded excited.

"Well," David said, "We were just looking around the area straight down from the hole when Betty noticed something on the bottom just to the left of where I was. As we came upon it, I couldn't believe my eyes. It was an old headstone off of a grave."

"What?" said Lilly and Ann at the same time.

"It was the headstone of a woman," Betty explained.

Lilly went weak in the knees and Ann was blown away, also.

"David, what else did you find?" Jim asked.

"Wait, please" said Lilly, "Tell us what was on the headstone? Was there a name?"

"Yes", replied Betty. "The name was that of a woman thirty one years old, Rebecca Jean Collins."

Ann said she wanted to know when the woman died, if that was on the headstone.

"It was 1920, and she was the wife of Joshua." Betty replied.

Ann moved closer to Lilly and whispered. "Did you hear the date of her death, Lilly?" "That was our ghost that appeared on the boat this morning, wasn't it?"

Lilly replied, "I think so."

David said it was easy to read after Betty cleaned the stone off. Don had been for a walk on the other side of the island and on his return, Brenda yelled, "Don guess what they found at the bottom of the lake."

"What?" he asked.

"They found the headstone of a woman."

"Wow!" said Don. They decided to go back to the houseboat and drop off the girls. Then take the diving equipment back to the marina. While the guys were gone Lilly told Ann that they must tell the others about the ghost of the young woman that appeared early this morning. Ann agreed and said that it had to be this Rebecca.

Lilly agreed with her that the weeping ghost was that of the lady the headstone related to. As the girls were busy preparing a snack for the guys. They noticed the book that Lilly had lain on the table wasn't there. Lilly looked for the book out on the front of the houseboat. They looked everywhere to no avail.

Lilly went to the back of the boat to check it out, when all of a sudden she smelled the scent of orange blossoms. It was faint at first, but as she stood there, the scent became overpowering. She knew that Rebecca was close. Still she didn't appear to Lilly. Just as Lilly was coming around the corner at the front of the boat she saw her book laying on the floor next to the chair the ghost, Rebecca, had sat in this morning. There was the orange blossom scent in the air.

Lilly picked up the book and called to the others that she had found the book. They came out to where she was and asked where she found it. Lilly pointed to the floor in front of her. They had been in so much of a hurry to find the book that it just hit them this moment. The orange blossom scent was thick in the air.

They looked at each other and Lilly told them, "She's been with us since I went to the back of the boat."

Brenda was suddenly conscious of a vague feeling of uneasiness. Her heart was pounding and her throat was becoming very dry.

Lilly and Ann also felt a sudden thickness in the air. Betty saw the woman taking form in front of them and knew she had better take a seat before she collapsed.

Rebecca Jean Collins stood in front of them with her hand holding the locket she wore around her neck. Lilly was the first to speak to the ghost of Rebecca. She had read and heard many times that you should ask what it is that they want. Most of the time you will receive an answer.

"What is it that you want from us?" Lilly ask Rebecca. They waited but she said nothing, just this sad look and the sound of unbearable pain. It was the kind of sound you couldn't stand to hear for long. It echoed through your soul.

"Please let us help you, Rebecca. That is your name, isn't it?" Lilly waited but nothing happened.

Rebecca seemed to glide over to the book Lilly had put down on the chair. She picked it up with the pages open to where it was the other morning before they moved out of the cove where they had seen the vision of the young man. Rebecca's weeping grew even louder and with the increase, it sounded more desperate, as if someone was tearing her heart out.

It became almost deafening to the ears of the others. Lilly reached for the book. Rebecca turned and looked at her and let it be removed from her hand. Lilly glanced at the pages and noticed that it was same pages that she had marked from before. Ann moved to Lilly's side so she could read the pages at the same time. As Ann moved, Rebecca stopped weeping.

The others wondered what was happening now. Rebecca moved to Ann, moved right through her as a matter of fact. As she passed through, Ann became weak and cold. Rebecca had disappeared but Ann was still weak and cold, even though it was in the nineties outside. She felt as if she was going to pass out.

The other girls rushed to help Lilly with Ann. They sat her down and Betty went to get her a glass of ice tea. Ann reached for the book and began to read out loud to the girls. Lilly had read and re-read the pages.

Now with Ann reading it to them it became clear. Both of the spirits were somehow related. How, she wasn't quite sure, but the pages talked of the burial of spirits and the separation of those spirits.

Betty still felt uneasy and as if the air around her had changed. She wasn't sure about what was happening to her friend, as she sat the glass of tea down next to Ann. What initially was not much more than uneasiness, a slight chill, proceeded to grow well beyond that into a terror, which froze her whole being. Betty looked over at Ann and in that instant knew why.

In a whisper, Betty cried, "Ann!" The others looked at the same time. Ann was ghostly white and her face was that of Rebecca.

"Oh, God, What does this mean?" Betty asked. "What do we do to help her?"

Out of Ann's mouth came a terrifying moaning sound, then the word, "Joshua."

Lilly knew they must do something but like the others, was spellbound, not knowing if they started to Ann's rescue if Rebecca would harm her. Rebecca spoke again, crying desperately, "Joshua."

Lilly had decided to take Ann's hand and as the contact with Lilly and Ann took place, Rebecca's face disappeared and Ann was returning to normal. Betty and Brenda joined Lilly in touching Ann. Rubbing her arms, they were still cool to the touch. Betty called to Ann.

After about five minutes Ann became herself.

"What happen to me?" she asked. Everyone brought a chair close to her and Lilly told her what had taken place just minutes before. Ann sat quietly for a while. "We must help Rebecca find Joshua. That's exactly what we have to do," Ann told the others.

It seemed like hours before the guys returned to the houseboat. Betty went to the back of the boat to meet the men as they pulled up along side the houseboat to tie the runabouts down. She asked them to come out on the front deck and join the other girls in a glass of ice tea. They agreed and said that sounded like a winner.

Jim walked through the galley to the front of the Stardust and the girls. Betty handed him a tall glass of tea and Jim thanked her with the remark, "This is just what the doctor ordered. It sure is getting unbearably hot today."

As he talked he noticed the girls were kind of quiet. He took a chair next to Ann, sat down and leaned over to give her a kiss. "What's my best girl been doing while I was away?" he asked Ann while taking her hand in his. Ann just looked at him and smiled, but by this time the others were joining the party.

David straightened up in his chair and admitted to himself that something was going on with the girls. Either the heat was getting to them or something was wrong. He looked over in Betty's direction. He knew his wife very well and she seemed to be a little on edge to him.

Lilly waited till all were settled down before she informed them of what had occurred since they had left to take back the equipment to the marina.

She started by telling them that they had a visitor while they were at the marina. John asked, "Who?"

Before she could answer David jumped in to say, "I hope you girls didn't have trouble with some wise guys trying to have fun, did you?"

He looked at Betty for the answer. Lilly didn't wait for Betty to answer him, she just started the story. "We had a visit from Rebecca Jean Collins while you were gone to take the equipment back."

Jim leaned back in his chair and laughed at this. "Okay, tell me, did you girls ask her for tea?"

John said to Lilly, "Your visit with her must not have gone very well at all because you girls were not your joyful selves when we returned."

Lilly shook her head at John and went right on with her story. "You see my book was missing and I went looking for it when Rebecca appeared to us on the front of the houseboat here, in the chair you are now setting in Jim. She also, at one point, took possession of Ann's body and spoke through Ann.

Jim twisted in his seat. He was getting a little concerned about where all this was going. He was afraid for his wife's well being. She had never been a believer in spiritualism. Never had they had the belief that spirits of the dead communicate or manifest their presence to the living. So why would Ann allow this to happen to her now?

"Honey, Why do you believe you were possessed by this Rebecca person?" Jim asked. "Jim, please try to understand that I didn't even know that it was happening to me at the time it did. Honey, it did happen and please let Lilly finish, okay?"

Lilly went on to tell about what Ann had said while in Rebecca's control. John got up and walked over to the railing and looked down into the water. He said that he couldn't believe this was really going on. But now that it had and they all knew of it, just what did it mean to them and should they maybe move from this area.

David sat inpatient wanting to take control of the situation. He loved a mystery, in fact this was his life. He was a good detective and this whole occurrence needed to be investigated. Betty told them she was the first to see that Rebecca had taken over Ann's body. She didn't want this to happen again because it left Ann totally exhausted and weak all over. She was cold as ice when they reached her after Rebecca had left her body. It took time for her to come back to them.

"What do you mean, for her to come back to you?" Jim asked, with a deep concern for his wife's welfare.

"Well, see, she was in a daze and her eyes were closed and she was icy cold, quite pale in color. We rubbed her hands and arms, and called her name several times before we got a response from her." replied Betty.

"How are you feeling at this moment?" Jim asked Ann but he wasn't sure she would answer him truthfully. Ann was conscious of the tension in the air. Everyone was waiting for her to answer. She knew that her answer had to be one of reassurance for all of them.

"I'm fine now, I'm even a bit hungry." Jim shrugged and said "I suppose it's harmless enough, but we can't be sure of it, can we? What will Rebecca try next time?"

David couldn't wait any longer he had to take charge now. He was twisting in his seat; this was it, he couldn't take any more. He knew what had to be done and with their help they could free Rebecca Collins forever.

David stood up, walked over to Ann and asked her if she knew where the map was. She told him it in the top drawer next to the sink. "Well, all of you sit still and I will tell you what we must do to get free of these spirits."

Brenda and Don listened to them and at the very same time glanced over at each other. As calmly as she could she said, "Guys, we have two spirits, remember. We don't even know if they are connected in any way to each other."

At that moment, David came back out on the sun deck. He walked over to the picnic table and put the map down.

"Okay, gather round and I'll show you what I found last time I looked at the map."

They moved to where they could all see the map. David began by showing them the counties that were marked on the map. "As you can see we are right now in between two counties. And this is where we found Rebecca's headstone. See anything different marked on this map than newer ones?"

John said "No", but as he worded it he saw the little crosses marked on the map at the point just yards away from where they had found Rebecca's headstone. "If I'm seeing right and I think I am, we have a cemetery that lies under the water."

"That's right," David told John. "When I looked at the map the other day I noticed the crosses and I read on the other side of the map that these crosses are markings of cemeteries. There are three cemeteries under the water if this map is right." He showed them where the other two were. "So knowing that, we just need to find out which county Rebecca is from, go to the courthouse and check the records. We can find all the information about her and her husband. Then maybe it will lead us to where her husband was buried. Maybe this check of the records will give us a hint of what Rebecca is trying to tell us. We can see how much we can discover about her life. Now all we need is to divide up into two groups and go to it, right?"

They all agreed, but just as they looked up from the map there on the front of the houseboat was Rebecca. This time all of them saw her. She was standing there looking at them. For the first time she wasn't weeping, but none of them noticed at the time.

"Oh, shit, I don't believe this", Jim said taking the nearest chair he could fine to sit in. Lilly went to move to where Rebecca was and just as she got maybe three steps from the table Rebecca raised her hand and pointed to the map.

Betty had a strange feeling that something was about to happen. This time her feeling of threat, danger, and dread was quite unmistakable.

Lilly asked Rebecca what she was pointing to. Rebecca seemed to be trying to communicate with them but to no avail. She swiftly moved to the table where she laid her finger on the spot where she wanted them to look. The only thing was her finger was not at the spot where her headstone was found. Lilly and David marked the area and as David put the mark on the map Rebecca started to weep again. There was a sudden chill in the air and the wind began to pick up.

The weeping stopped and Rebecca disappeared. Betty knew that now something was happening. The others sat waiting to see if Rebecca would appear again or what might happen next, but Betty was really getting upset with every moment that went by, feeling the air and wind change. She looked around at the others and then at Ann.

"NO", Betty cried out loud, "not again." They all turned their attention to Betty. They saw that she was looking at Ann. Their attention went directly to Ann wondering what was up. She was setting in a chair next to Jim, with her eyes fixed and her face was turning pale white again. To their amazement Ann's face was taking on the face of Rebecca.

Jim's heart was in his throat. He reached over to touch his wife but as he laid his hand on her's she pulled free and pushed his chair and him away from her with great force. As a strong man might do. Jim called Ann's name, stood up and started to take hold of Ann, but before he could reach her, Rebecca lifted him off the floor and into mid air. Just two feet in the air, that was enough for everyone to take notice that the atmosphere was one of violence, not one of peacefulness like Rebecca had demonstrated before.

John had laid his fishing rods and tackle box upon the top of the boat when they had come in from fishing earlier today. The force of power was so great coming from Rebecca that the fishing rods and pieces of other tackle were being tossed into the water.

Lilly was deeply concerned about what was taken place. She knew that she should try to calm the spirit of Rebecca, so she softly called to her. "Rebecca, please put him down. He meant you no harm. You occupy his wife's body and he is gravely concerned about what you are doing to her. He is afraid you will harm her."

Rebecca slowly put him down and as she did the wind decreased and the air wasn't as foreboding. Jim sat back down in the chair feeling a deep sense of helplessness. After she let him go, she walked back over to the map, put her finger on the spot where she had it before and in her voice not Ann's said just one word; "Joshua". She then turned around to look at Jim.

Ann was aware that something was happening to her body but there wasn't a thing she could do to stop Rebecca from entering her. Slowly Ann collapsed onto the floor. Betty and Jim were up out of their chairs and at Ann's side helping her to a chair. She was like before, weak and cold to the touch.

Lilly went to get some tea for her to drink while Jim held Ann's hands and tried to talk to her. Ann was aware of everything but too weak to make any sense out of Rebecca entering her body again. The first time Ann wasn't aware of Rebecca possessing her. Now the whole episode was clear.

When Ann gathered enough strength to speak she asked, "Why do you think Rebecca chose me to possess? Why not one of you?"

Lilly said that from the books that she had read sometimes its the person's ability to accept the unknown and then again it could be because the spirit and the person have something in common. "After all, Ann, Rebecca is or, should I say, was your age when she died, wasn't she?" Lilly said.

"I see what you mean but I really don't want this to happen to me again because it takes all my strength away. I feel so weak and drained after she leaves my body."

"Honey this is not and I repeat is not going to happen to you again if I can help it." Jim told her with great concern for her health.

David explained to Jim that she got violent because he tried to stop her from getting her message over to us. "She has told us without a doubt where Joshua is, but I don't understand how he could be where she says he is. Maybe he had an accident on the lake and was drowned. Maybe we need to find out what Joshua was doing where Rebecca has indicated. If I'm the least bit right, something has happened to Joshua and he was our ghost in the other channel. If we go to the courthouse and library in both of these counties we surely will find something on them, don't you think?" asked David.

"Yes", they all said together. "Well, lets start out early in the morning and see what the Collins' family secrets are," David replied.

DAY SIX

Sunrise came faster than normal to them it seemed. That was because all on board the Stardust had slept soundly the whole night. All had dreams of their own, but not restless like a few other nights. No one was disturbed by spirits from the other world. After they had breakfast and David laid out their plan of action for the day, they loaded up and off they went in two different directions to find the records of Rebecca and Joshua Collins, whatever that may be or wherever it might take them.

Jim pulled up in front of the Jonesville Court House about a half hour later. It was a small town of approximately eighteen hundred people. The Court House itself was in the middle of town. It was a large two story red brick building, with four white columns in the front. Its appearance was like a lot of older buildings in the South. The town was clean and well-kept. About twenty stores altogether made up the town.

Lilly, Jim, Ann and Brenda went up the walk and through the double doors together. They had to split up to find all the information as quickly as possible. The others, David, Betty, Don and John were entering the town of Summerfield. It was almost like Jonesville, but not as well-kept.

The building was old and unpainted and showed much decay. Only about eight to nine hundred people lived here. Most of the town's people were or had been miners, but were now in the older age group. There just didn't seem to be that many young people around.

But to the surprise of all, as they rounded the corner to the library they were impressed. There was this beautiful white frame three story house which was set back on a broad green lawn that was surrounded by blooming bushes and carpets of wildflowers in and around the tall oak trees that must have been at least two times as old as the house. This was truly the most cherished building in the whole town.

They parked and went into the library. It was just as impressive on the inside. There was a lady of about sixty years of age with gray hair and a little on the plump side, a grandmotherly type, who came to greet them. She directed them to the places they needed to look. A card catalog was not needed here. It was modern and the newspapers had been put on slides.

This was Betty's job. She would go back as far as she could and see if anything was mentioned about Rebecca and Joshua in the papers.

David went over to talk to the lady in charge of the library. She seemed the type to know something about the people of the community. David told her he was interested in the Collins family. She asked which Collins, there were at least three different Collins families and they weren't related. David said that he was primarily interested in the family of Joshua and Rebecca Jean Collins. "Did you know of them?" he wondered.

She sat quietly for a while and then replied yes she knew of the Joshua Collins family but if she wasn't mistaken they were all gone. David ask what she meant by,"all gone".

The lady's name was Mary, and she replied that "all gone" meant dead.

David felt despair at that moment and decided to see what the others had come up with. He went over to Betty to see if she had come up with anything. She hadn't yet but there was still more to look through. On the other hand Don and John had been looking through some old pictures of some of the town's people and much to their surprise, before them was a portrait of their mystery ghost, Rebecca J. Collins.

In the picture she wore the very same silver locket. It was around her neck, but in this picture she was showing the locket off, because it was opened and the photo inside was that of a young man, Joshua. Don knew it had to be him because it was the face he had seen on the houseboat.

He was struck by the uncanny likeness of the ghost and this picture. There were other portraits of the Collins family. One was of a child, a girl. There was nothing else about the child. He wondered if maybe this was their child. If so she could still be alive today, maybe even still in this area. Don showed the findings to David. He was pleased with the news.

David took the book over to Mary to see if maybe this would jog her memory. He asked her if she knew this lady, that she was the woman that they were trying to find information on. "This is Rebecca Collins and the locket has a photo of who we think is Joshua. There is a child here also and we hope this child is theirs and that she is still here in town or in a town near here. Would you take a look and see if maybe you know of them."

Mary glanced up at the photos and to her amazement she did know of the child and the parents. "This little girl is Rebecca's daughter. Her name was Grace. I'm sorry to tell you that they all are dead. They were killed in a car accident. They were coming home from a family party when another car ran them off the road and over the cliff. They were killed instantly. It was a terrible shame. They were so young and so much in love. They are buried in the Collins family cemetery, just west of here."

David said," Bingo".

He went out to the car and got the map and came back into the library. "Mary would you take a look at this map and show me where the cemetery is in connection with this town?" David asked. All of them gathered around to see where Mary would say was the spot.

She looked at the map and it took a little time for her to show them on this map because of the lake. She told them that to her recollection it should be about right here and she pointed to the area where they had spent the first night on the lake.

Mary told them that she thought the Corps of Engineers for the Tennessee Valley Authority had moved the cemetery but she couldn't be sure, that maybe they needed to talk with one of the engineers or better yet, she knew a man that worked on the project when it was first started and he lives right here in town.

"He was one who helped organize the moving of the cemeteries that had to be relocated because of the lake. His name is Tom Mullins and he lives on Hilltop Street. You go down to the end of this block and make a right which is Elm, take it all the way to the end and that will be Hilltop. Tom has a big old house that is painted white with brown trim and a big swing in the yard. You can't miss it."

David gathered everyone and they headed for the Mullins house. Betty felt overcome by a sudden rush of sympathy for the Collins family. She understood Rebecca better now. David was pulling up in front of the Mullins house. Mary had given them good directions to get there.

Don was very excited about the whole situation, to know that this man may be the one with all the answers for them.

Samantha Moss 71

They all descended upon the house. The front door was open, so they knew someone had to be at home. David knocked and a women's voice called, "I'm coming". A lady in her late seventy's answered the door. She asked what they wanted.

David replied, "I'm looking for Mr. Tom Mullins, is he here?"

"Oh yes, he's here somewhere" she said. "He was out back resting the last I saw him. Just go around back and look, he's there somewhere."

They went around the house and on the way Betty said, "I really hope this man can help. He must be in his seventy's, like the lady that answered the door. He may have lost some of his memory. Lets just pray he hasn't forgot about the Collins family."

As they approached the back yard, there in the big old swing that hung from the largest old oak tree they had ever seen was this very old man with snow white hair and dark rugged looking skin. He had to be near eighty years old. He was sleeping they thought but as they approached him, his eyes opened and he sat up.

David said, "Hello, Mr. Mullins?" He got out of the swing and reached out his hand to David and replied, "Yes, I'm Tom Mullins, what can I do for you people." He made a motion for them to sit down. He looked at Betty and said, "You sit with me in this here swing."

She moved over to the swing. It was a beautiful old swing that would seat two or three people. "I made this swing", he said as Betty joined him. "Now young man, what do you want with old Tom?"

"Mr. Mullins, we're trying to find some information about the Joshua Collins family. Do you remember them?" Tom thought for a while before he answered. Don was holding his breath hoping with all his heart that this man could remember something.

"There are many Collins families in the area. I can't recall Joshua Collins." Betty spoke before David and said, "Tom, we know that Joshua and Rebecca Collins died a long time ago, but we are trying to find out where they where laid to rest. They also had a child that died with them. Don't you remember them at all?"

By this time Tom was smiling, "Oh yes, yes, I recall Rebecca because she was a Mullins before she married Joshua Collins. That's been a long time back girl, why do you people want to know about them?"

David knew that he must be very careful how he answered Tom about this. "We are renting a houseboat for the week and the lady at the marina gave us this old map that showed three cemeteries that were covered over with water when the lake was formed. Do you know anything about these cemeteries?"

David didn't tell him how he knew about the Collins' being buried there, if indeed they were buried there. He just dropped that issue. John said to Tom, "We hear you were an engineer working on the lake project when it was built."

"Yeah, You got that right," Tom answered. "You see, I was the first man in this area to be hired to help with the lake. I knew most of the families in the area and they needed to acquire some of the land that was used to make the lake. You are also right about the cemeteries that were there at the bottom of the lake. There were three to my recollection and you know my memory just isn't as good as it use to be. We moved them to another area. You see, we had to get the families to agree to let us relocate them graves. These were little family plots. One was three different families if I remember right", Tom said.

They heard the screen door at the back of the house shut and as they looked around Mrs. Mullins was coming out to them with a large pitcher of lemonade and glasses. As she approached them she said, "It's hot out here today and I thought you people might like something cold to drink."

Betty thanked her for the thought. The lemonade was refreshing. Mrs. Mullins took a chair next to John. David went on to ask Tom, "Did you move all of the graves to new locations?"

"Well I'll tell you now, there is always some graves that aren't marked in these parts. People here bouts just don't always mark graves of their loved ones, not to say they forget where they are, you see. I'd say we probably got ninety six percent of them. Some of the graves couldn't be moved because we couldn't get permission to move them. Either the family was all dead and gone or we just couldn't talk the nearest kin into giving us the permission we needed to move them."

"What happened to the ones that weren't moved?" Don asked.

"It's simple son. The relatives wanted them to stay right where they were laid to rest. But there weren't many we had like that. The only thing in a situation like this was to worry about the ones that wasn't marked and had no family to tell us where they were. I've lived here all my life and I'm not sure we got all of them."

"Tom, did you get permission to move the Collins family?" Don asked.

"Sure we did, we moved them, but I'm not sure where at this moment."

"Tom," Mrs. Mullins said, "Don't you recall that you didn't move Joshua Collins or his little girl. You only moved Rebecca."

Tom sat thinking. No one said a thing for quite awhile. They didn't want to rush him. But were anxious to hear his answer to what Mrs. Mullins had just said happened.

"You know Mother, I think you're right about this. We did move only one of them and that had to be Rebecca."

David asked, "Why would you have moved only one and why would it have been Rebecca?"

"I really can't tell you that because I don't recall. Mother do you know how that happened?" Tom asked his wife a little upset with himself.

"I don't recall what the reason was at the time but maybe we can remember, later," replied his wife. Betty knew they had almost got the information they needed. She knew that at Tom's age they shouldn't tire him anymore today. Maybe if they gave him some time to think about this he would recall more later.

Betty stood up and thanked them for their hospitality. "Maybe we could come back tomorrow and talk with you again, Tom." she said.

Tom got up, shook their hands and said he would try to recall what did take place with the Collins family.

After they returned to the car David said, "We need to come back and see if he can shed some more light on this. We are so close to the answers, I feel."

They headed back to the houseboat and to see if the others had learned anything.

Lilly, Jim, Ann, and Brenda were getting ready to leave Jonesville. They had no luck at all finding out about the Collins family of Joshua. They had talked to a few people that worked in the courthouse and they told Lilly that it was possible to find out what they were looking for in Summerfield.

Jim was glad to hear this because that meant that David would have something when he and the others returned to the Stardust. The only real information they had received was that the office of the Corp of Engineers should give them some information about the cemeteries.

The office was on their way out town so they stopped to see if maybe something could be found out. They parked outside the office and decided to all go in together, a woman greeted them. They told her they were trying to find out information about the cemeteries that had to be moved when the lake was formed.

She said, "Some of the old records were in the upstairs file room. We are required to keep all the information that was believed to be important. You can go through them if you want, but they can't leave this building."

"We understand", said Lilly. She lead them to the upstairs room where the records were kept. It was like the rest of the building, with dark heavy paneling that reached from floor to ceiling, with bookcases along one side of the room. The ceiling was beautiful with a mural of paintings around the four corners of the ceiling. "You may use this area here to examine the records. There are about four filing cabinets with the information you are looking for."

They each took a cabinet and started in. Brenda came across the file of Joshua Collins in minutes. She called the others over and they looked through the records. They came across the record of how the authorities could not get the Collins' family to authorize the removal of the graves to a new location. They had tried a few times and had failed. The graves would stay where they were as far as the authorities were concerned.

Brenda said she didn't have confidence in the report. Something wasn't right. They continued to read the reports. Nothing really important was showing up in the records. They were about to give up when just then the big heavy oak door to the room swung open. They looked up and saw no one come through it.

Next there were strong heavy footsteps moving in the room near them but, it was only the sound they heard. It went right to the filing cabinets. They looked at each other knowing someone was in the room with them. There was a shrill sound made as a drawer of one of the cabinets opened. Jim found Ann was trembling violently. Tears had begun to form in her eyes. He knew she was trying to control them.

He put his hand on her shoulder and stood up to go over to the cabinet that now stood open.

As he reached the cabinet, the footsteps moved in the direction of the oak door. They followed the sound as it went through the door and it came shut again. Everyone was on edge but Ann was sitting there stiff as could be.

"It's okay", Brenda told Ann. "It's gone now." Ann shook her head in agreement but still looked like she was ready to explode. Jim looked down into the cabinet and a single file was pulled up for him to take out. The front of the file read Rebecca Mullins. Jim couldn't believe his eyes. He was really starting to believe in ghosts.

Something was definitely leading them to the right places, that was for sure. He took the file over and laid it on the table to examine. "Lilly, you girls might have a Rebecca Mullins not Collins on our boat."

"That can't be", Brenda replied. "Betty and David found her headstone remember?" "Yes, but then explain this file that was pulled for us to look at," Jim responded a little agitated. The file had four sheets of paper in it. One was a letter from the Mullins family wanting the grave to be moved to another area. They had a family plot in the next county and the lake wasn't to extend to that area, so they were to move Rebecca to another grave site.

The next paper was the removal form and it was signed by Ralph and Iris Mullins. They were her parents. They didn't have room for the three graves so only the grave of Rebecca could be moved.

The last sheet of paper was dated twenty-five years after the lake was formed. At that time the lake was to be made much larger and this would again entail the removal of the cemetery of the Mullins family.

The important fact in this letter was that there wasn't any way they could find the living relatives of the family to now get the permission required to move the graves. Ralph and Iris had passed away by this time. So the lake authorities left the graves where they were. There was a map on the wall that showed the whole lake.

Jim went over to the map to see if he could pin point the spot where the Mullins plot was located by the letter he had in his hand. It wasn't very clear because some of the details were in metes and bounds description. When he had done his best, he called the others over to take a look.

He found that it was right where David and Betty had located the headstone. "We have a major breakthrough here, crew", Jim told them. "We now know that Rebecca has been moved from Joshua and wants to be back with him where she belongs. That's why she is not at rest," Lilly told them. "And that's why her ghost still remains earthbound. Lets take the information back with us to show the others."

They ran copies of the papers and headed back to the houseboat feeling a lot easier.

It was late afternoon when David and his team returned to the Stardust. The others hadn't made it back yet. David thought this was a good sign that they had discovered something. On the other hand Betty was worried that maybe something was wrong. She didn't tell David, Don or John of her apprehension. She was fearful and was trying hard to comprehend the meaning of the whole situation in its entirety, wondering where this would lead them. It was just so hard to grasp.

This lake was so wonderful that one would never imagine something as frightening as they had experienced happening. They could never tell anyone what had been going on for fear they would be laughed at or thought to be liars. This could be as bad for them as for people who tell about seeing UFO's.

David, John and Don decided to get some tea to drink and go out on the back sun deck to relax till the others returned. Betty was still meditating on all this when a loud noise brought her back to the present. David was pouring another glass of ice tea. The ice cubes made the loud noise.

David had been studying Betty for a while before the ice made the noise that caught her attention. "You look exhausted," his voice showing signs of concern. "I'm a little tried from all the running around and tension of wanting to find out about our spirit. I'll be all right after a good night's sleep," she replied back to David, wondering if anyone of them would be the same as they were before this vacation.

It had affected all of them in some way, she knew. The others returned to the Stardust approximately two and a half hours later than David and his team. They brought the runabout up along side the houseboat and John helped to tie it up. They were all beaming from head to toe, so excited about the news they had come up with. Brenda was the first to board the Stardust and as soon as she was on board she started telling them, "We have great news."

She was dancing all around. David put a hand on her shoulder and told her to keep it till they all are able to hear what she have come up with.

Betty chimed in, "Wait till we have dinner and then we will pull out all the information and see what we have on the Collins family."

"You just won't believe what we have," said Brenda.

"Hold it for now!" instructed Don.

David knew that with the excitement that Brenda was showing, they had found some important information. He was like Brenda in that he would like to skip dinner and go right to the information at hand.

Dinner was prepared and all the while Brenda paced the floor. Don said watching her for a time, "Brenda, your restlessness makes me nervous. I really can't bear it when you pace like this."

Brenda stopped, startled by Don's words. "Don, you can eat anytime but we want to find out about the spirit on board this boat and now that we have something, you want to eat! Well, I don't want to wait, forever. Hurry up so we can get started with the issue at hand," Brenda said as she started to pace again.

They did hurry and finish eating in record time. None of them really wanted to waste time that wasn't necessary.

Lilly told the girls to clean off the table first and for David to get the map and lay it out on the table. All gathered around in their chairs. Jim had the papers they had run copies of and laid them out in front of David. David asked Jim if he wanted to explain the papers.

Jim said, "No, I really think you all should read them yourselves and then we will talk about what they mean, or what we think they mean."

Each one of the papers were read and then laid aside. Betty suddenly felt less like reading anymore and more like taking a shower and getting some rest. Yet she would avoid any possibility of being left alone in the back cabin while the others went on discussing the papers and what was next on the game plan. She really felt like the day would never end.

After Jim and his team, consisting of Lilly, Ann and Brenda, told what had transpired on their search. David informed them of what was happening with his team and what was uncovered.

"We need to go see Tom Mullins again early in the morning. I sincerely hope this old man can remember something else that may shed some more light on the subject. We know that Rebecca's grave was with her husband and little girl and that she was moved to the Mullins family plot, which took her from the ones she loved and wanted to be with. So now that we know all this what can we do to help Rebecca to reunite with her family?" David asked and waited for their response.

No one dared to attempt to introduce a method to reunite them because they all knew that it had to mean taking Rebecca's grave and moving it back to the area where Joshua and Grace were. That was not possible and they all knew it would be out of the question. How would they even go about such a matter?

Brenda's next words astonished them, because what was unspoken she put into spoken words and now they had to respond. "There is no sense in this idea because the authorities would not let us or anyone go down and disturb a grave at this late date. I believe that there are some sensible things we can do that should help heal or lighten the spirit of Rebecca. We can tell her that her family is near here and that they are at rest, that she must let go and take peace in the fact that they are very close to her," Brenda finished saying as they got hit with the scent of heavy orange blossoms.

They all turned and looked around the room, while Lilly asked, "Rebecca, are you here?"

They knew that she was or maybe had been up till that time. Rebecca didn't respond to Lilly. They waited for a while before Jim said that there was only one thing they had to try and that was to get help to move the grave.

"I suppose I agree with your preposterous suggestion, but, and that's a big, BUT… what would we tell the authorities was the reason behind the removal of this old grave, tell me gang?" David asked, feeling defeated before he had even started.

Betty knew with the kind of people she believed the Mullins couple to be, since her talk with them, that they might listen and do what they could to help with a cause like this. After all it was a member of their family.

"David", Betty said, "If we went to Tom and his wife and explained the facts gently, don't you think they could help with getting the authorities to go along with us?"

"Betty, come on, be sensible. You know as well as anyone of us that we can't tell them about the ghosts. No one will believe this kind of thing. Ghosts, tell me another story they will say 'These people come down here from the North and see spirits. That's a good laugh.'" David just shook his head. "I really think we need time to come up with a few more suggestions."

Betty couldn't take anymore for the evening. She was so exhausted that nothing was making sense. She thought about the scent of orange blossoms they had smelled earlier. She, like the others, was aware that Rebecca was there but that she didn't feel it necessary to appear to them. Had she approved of the next step or was she really satisfied with the thought that her family was near? Would she go along with just knowing this?

Betty thought, I must try to stop thinking about her and get some much-needed rest. She stood up and informed the others that they all needed to go to bed for the night and by morning things may look different to all of them. Jim said it sounded great, he was tried of thinking about spirits, graves, and the like. "Lets see which one of us can hit the bed first."

Betty was already on her way to the bathroom (the head they call it on board ship) and would be the first to bed and asleep. They all were in bed and asleep in record time, all having their own dreams of the day's events, or was it the night's events? During the night Rebecca visited them. She hadn't awakened anyone of them but it was because she was doing other things that they would discover in the morning as they arose and talked to each other. Rebecca's powers were very strong after all and just how strong, they would soon find out.

DAY SEVEN

The sun was high in the sky by the time they managed to awake and get dressed and ready for their first cup of coffee. It seems like when you are out like this coffee smells and tastes better than when you are at home. It was definitely going to be another hot day. The sun was pouring through the galley windows and by this time it was becoming quite sticky inside the cabin already.

Lilly made coffee and the smell was delightful. The other girls started breakfast. Lilly ask Don if the front sun deck would be a bit more comfortable.

"Yes, it would make things more enjoyable for all of us because we would have a bit more air stirring out there. So what are you waiting for? Toss me a dish towel and I'll clean off the table for you." Don replied.

When breakfast was ready, everyone sat down at the table across from each other. "Did you sleep well, David?" Betty asked. He nodded that he did, as he took a bite of toast. "I hope all of you slept well!" she added. "Because I must have dreamed all night. The thing is I normally don't remember what I dream about, but this time I remember everything that happened."

Lilly hesitated pouring her coffee, telling Betty that she also had dreams all night but they were not nightmares like she had been having. By now all of them agreed on one thing about last night: they had all dreamed!

Betty began to feel the uneasiness that was always present when Rebecca was around or when she had caused something to happen. This was no different, it had Rebecca's name written all over it. She listened to the others tell almost the same story that she did. When one of then stopped telling it one of the others would pick up right where the story left off and continue right on with it.

Now she wondered if they did dream or if maybe they all were somehow hypnotized by the spirit of Rebecca. Perhaps they where shown the dream, as if placed in their minds. She knew Rebecca could be that powerful if she wanted. Lilly was always a bit clairvoyant and this ability to perceive things was growing stronger as time on board the houseboat with Rebecca grew.

Lilly knew Rebecca was responsible for the dream last night. It was a sign from her of what she expected from them, what they must do about helping her get back to the husband and child she was laid to rest with. Lilly just wasn't sure how they were going to accomplish this task. Somehow they had to return Rebecca to her beloved Joshua.

David got up from the table to go to the galley to get another glass of water. As he was returning to the sun deck he happened to glance over at the place where they kept the maps and other papers they had brought back from yesterday's investigation. David walked over to take a closer look at what was on top the papers because from where he was standing it looked to be a shiny object.

David went weak in the knees as he gazed upon the object and the papers. He regained his composure, picked up the papers and the shiny object and headed for the others on the front sun deck of the Stardust.

They were talking small talk as David approached them. Setting down the things he carried in the center of the table, he caught everyone's attention. "Well, it is apparent that a number of things were presented to us last night. First in our dreams and now by this. These were left for us to find this morning."

Their eyes focused on the silver object in the center of the papers first. To their amazement it was the lovely locket wore by Rebecca. Under it were the words in old script writing; MOVE ME!! Without saying a word they all sat and thought about this and what was about to become the greatest task of their lives.

Cold chills ran up Jim's arms and he felt he was becoming sick to his stomach. He had gone along with all that was happening but still not taking it seriously… until now!

Ann leaned over on his arm. Her breath was hot to his neck. He still was cold and this caused the chilling again. Suddenly Jim found the strength to move. He stood up and walked toward the very front of the boat, stumbled and almost fell, but regained his balance.

When he reached the front of the boat, he leaned through the railing and vomited. Never had he felt so sick. By this time they all were feeling a little weak and sick. When he was almost finished, Ann was by his side rubbing his back. Her voice soft, she asked if he was better.

"I was sick," Jim said weakly. "Just really sick. It's over, I'm okay now." They walked back over to the group and sat down.

Brenda asked quietly but urgently, "What do we do now? We really didn't have anything very much to convince anyone of the presence of Rebecca before, but she has just given us all the proof we need. Lets all pull ourselves together and go pay a visit to Mr. Mullins, because as I see it he is our only link to getting the help we need to move the grave back where it belongs."

As they did the dishes, Ann told Betty she thought she would stay on board the Stardust and wait for their return. "All of us shouldn't show up at Mr. Mullins' house. He may become frightened of us, after he hears what we are asking of him. I think it would be better if some of us remained on board the boat."

"You're right about it frightening him if we show up and tell him our story. Maybe I will stay with you," Betty said.

Ann told her that since she was there the other day that she felt it was best that she go with them. After all she was a nurse and could see things in people that may tell them if he is taking the news about Rebecca Collins well.

"Do you know that you always make good sense?" Betty said taking a deep breath. Brenda had been listening to them. She told them that she would stay with Ann because it really seemed that they had been on the go every minute of every day since they had first arrived on this crazy vacation.

It came down to David, Betty , John and Lilly going to see Tom Mullins. The rest of them would wait on board the Stardust. So off they went with the papers and Rebecca's locket in hand to convince Tom that Rebecca Collins was a spirit that was still earthbound because she longed to be back with her beloved Joshua and Grace, that her spirit couldn't rest till they were all reunited again.

They would tell Tom of Joshua and how they had happened upon his spirit and that he also was still on this earth. Then they would pray that Tom and his wife would somehow be able to accept this fact and help move Rebecca's coffin back to the place she was first laid to rest.

They pulled up in front of the Mullins' house and David said he thought that he should do the talking at first. For the others to wait before saying anything. They agreed with David whole-heartedly.

David knocked on the door and Mrs. Mullins greeted them. "Good Morning, Mrs. Mullins. We would like to see Tom."

She invited them into a small room off the entry, somewhat like a sitting room. It was full of plants and furnished with white wicker. She invited them to sit down while she went to get Tom. David knew he must plan his words very carefully because of Tom's age.

After a long tension filled moment Tom appeared in the doorway. He walked in with a big smile on his face and said, "Mother told me it was you young folks. Sure glad to see you came back to see old Tom."

David stood up and shook his hand, then introduced Lilly and John. Tom said,"Glad to meet you Lilly, I met your husband yesterday." Tom went over and sat down in a chair next to where there was a small table with a pipe and tobacco. He started to light up just as Mrs. Mullins joined them.

"Tom, don't you dare light that there pipe up before you ask our guests if it would offend them."

"Hush Mother, they don't mind an old man smoking his pipe," as he looked around at them with a big grin on his face.

"That's okay Mrs. Mullins," David replied before anything else was said.

"I think you people should know that I did a great deal of thinking about the Collins family and Rebecca most of all last night. Kept Mother here up way past her bedtime." Tom laughed and then continued. "You city folk stay up late but down in these here hills we go to bed with the chickens. Why, we roll the streets up at eight o'clock in the evening around these parts, don't ya know!"

Betty thought how jolly this man was, his wife also, but what would happen when David told them why they were here and what they wanted them to help with? She wondered how Tom would react to it.

David started to twist in his seat. "Tom, since we talked to you yesterday a lot has happened to us. We would like you and your wife to hear us out and hopefully keep an open mind about what it is we are about to tell you. I don't know how you feel about such things as spirits or ghosts."

Tom reared back in his chair and said, "Well son, let me tell you that these dag-gone hills down here are alive with all kinds of ghost stories and we live close to God. I reckon you might say we live with ghosts all the time down here bouts in these parts. So, young man, I hope I set your mind at ease."

David breathed a sigh of relief. "Tom, you see we didn't believe in things like spirits and ghosts, whichever you may want to call them till we came down here on vacation. We have had the pleasure of meeting two spirits since that time."

Tom just sat listening to David all the while puffing on his pipe. Mrs. Mullins interrupted David to ask if she could get us some coffee. He told her that would be nice. This gave David a chance to think a second or two about how to explain Rebecca.

"We didn't believe in things like this, but now that we have been in the presence of these two spirits, we have learned a lot that we thought was impossible. Tom, we know who the two spirits are and what must be done to help put things back the way they were meant to be."

David went on to explain Rebecca's ghost and how she had communicated with all of them. Then David told Tom and his wife that after last night they knew only to well that they needed the help of the both of them.

Tom leaned back in his chair and ask, "Son you have been skirtin' around this story long enough, ain't you comin' to the point of this here purpose? I'm an old man and I sure ain't gettin' any younger waitin' for you to get to the place of how me and Mother here can help you young folks out."

David took a deep breath and said, "We know that the ghost of the woman is that of Rebecca Jean Collins."

Mrs. Mullins caught her breath, then in a soft whisper but loud enough for them to hear said, "Oh, Good Lord, poor child. I reckoned this was bout to happen. Them two young people were too much in love for anyone to move her grave from that of her husband. It was just crazy to move that grave."

Tom studied on it for a moment then went on, "They're a comin' back, ain't they? They want us to put them back the way it was. My lord, I don't see how we could find her grave and put it back since its under all that there water."

"Mr. Mullins, we know where the grave of Rebecca is, we're just not sure how to move it back to the other cove with Joshua. Or, if the authorities would go long with such a story as this one. Do you know how we could go about moving the grave without anyone knowing?" Lilly asked him.

"I reckon there is a way if you are sure that this ghost is that of Rebecca." Tom replied.

Then Mrs. Mullins ask them how they knew for sure who she was.

Betty had been carrying the locket and papers that Rebecca had left the message on. She laid it out on the wicker table in front of them. "This is just how we found these things this morning.," said Betty.

Tom picked up the locket and looked inside it, then handed it to his wife. "I think maybe we should wait till I kin check it out about moving the grave back with the people down at the court house. We don't want to get in all kinds of trouble," he said.

John told Tom that they only had a few days left of their vacation and that something should be done soon.

They got up to leave at this time, thanked the Mullins' for listening to them and that they would stop by first thing in the morning if that was okay. John also told Tom where the houseboat was anchored and if he needed to, he could come out and maybe see Rebecca for himself.

"I reckon that might be a good idea, to check out what you folks say." Tom replied.

"Well, we'll be off for now, Tom." David said as they walked to the door.

Meanwhile, Don and Brenda decided to go fishing in the other runabout while waiting for David and the others to come back from their visit with the Mullins. They baited their lines and out of the cove they went.

Slowly they moved around the shoreline not paying much attention to where they were. They had caught three nice bass and were really getting into fishing by this time. Don baited Brenda's fishing line because she hated to put bait on the hook, even though she loved to catch fish. So for a while they lost track of how far they had gone from the houseboat and what time it was. The farther they went the larger the fish seemed to get.

Ann had packed them a sandwich and something to drink. They drifted into a cove and over close to the bank where the trees hung over the water. Don dropped the anchor so they wouldn't drift too close to the shore. This was a perfect place to take a break and have their food. The trees cast a shade of about ten feet in the water and they needed it by this time because the sun was really beating down and it felt hotter because there was no breeze stirring.

They sat drinking and enjoying their sandwiches. As they talked small talk, Don asked Brenda if he could take a quick nap. He told her it was so wonderful feeling the breeze from the trees every once in a while and the quietness of the cove, that it was so relaxing he would love to just rest for a while. She was enjoying the shade as well, and the singing sounds of the birds in the trees, that she to would like to drift off for a while also.

Don fell asleep and so did Brenda. He slept for about twenty minutes and then a dream started or rather a nightmare seized him. He knew he was asleep; he realized it and could see himself asleep which was really strange. He was conscious of someone approaching him, looking at him.

Next the figure of the man climbed on board the boat, kneeled over Don's chest and seized him by the throat, with all the strength the man had, Don felt the man try to strangle him. He felt himself try to struggle, trying to push the man off him, but he couldn't move, feeling paralyzed by the dream. He tried to scream to wake Brenda but he couldn't. The person was crushing and suffocating him. Don was totally powerless against the dream's effect.

Suddenly he woke up in a panic, dripping with sweat and there was no one there. He looked around and saw no one anywhere around. The movement of the boat woke Brenda. She took one look at Don and knew something was wrong.

"What is it, Honey?" she asked.

"I'm okay now. I went to sleep and had a terrible dream that's all." he replied. He took a deep breath and smelled the fresh air, so soft and cool, full of the scents of the forest. It was invigorating and stimulated his senses. Yet the dream was still very much on his mind. He took a towel and wiped the sweat from his face. Brenda sat back and enjoyed the view and wished they had more times like this together.

"We had better head back to the houseboat don't you think?" Don asked Brenda. "Yes, I guess we must, but I wish we had more time together like this," she told him.

He went to the front of the boat to pull up the anchor when suddenly he shivered. It was not a shiver caused by a cool breeze on his hot skin but one of fright. He quickened his pace in pulling the anchor up. He felt someone was watching him. Brenda cleaned up the things from the lunch they had, not really paying any attention to Don.

Don felt so foolish because the dream had put his nerves on edge and he couldn't get the feelings to go away. He looked around the shoreline where they were and saw absolutely nothing. Pulling the anchor up was becoming more of a challenge. It was approximately thirty or forty feet down he knew but it felt like he was pulling up three anchors instead of one.

He wondered what was making it so heavy. The anchor itself had the weight of about twelve pounds. That was nothing to pull up. Don asked Brenda to help him with the anchor because he was getting exhausted. She laughed at this and went to help. She had pulled up anchors before and knew it wasn't hard to do. Don gave her the line and stepped back a couple of feet. "Set down Don and I will take care of the anchor.," she said.

He watched as she had no trouble in pulling the anchor up. It would take her awhile so he sat down. He again had the feeling that something or someone was watching him, was behind him. He swung around sharply but saw nothing, closed his eyes and told himself to relax that the dream was still bothering him.

As Brenda was bringing the anchor on board he got up to help her. After placing it in the lower storage area Don went to start the runabout and head back to the houseboat. The engine wouldn't start. He tried and tried with no luck.

"Is the battery down or something?" Brenda asked.

He checked the gauges and everything showed to be all right. They had charged the battery the other day at the Marina so they would be ready for the next few days of fishing.

This runabout belonged to Ann and Jim. They had the engine serviced before the trip down here so nothing should be wrong. He turned the key again, nothing, not even a spark from the engine. It was dead as dead could be.

"Don, the others don't know where we are, do they?" she asked.

"They know we headed east around the shore line but that's it. I don't even know how far we are from the houseboat," he announced. They sat in silence for quite some time. Each wondering what they should do next. Maybe, Don thought, the others will see that it's getting late and come looking for us. If they do that, it is a sure bet they will find us fast.

"Brenda, lets use this time to fish some more. If you want to I can get us over to shore and tie the boat up so we are not on the water." She told him that was a good idea.

Ann and Jim sat on the back sun deck of the Stardust enjoying the calm beauty of the lake. Having this time together was what the doctor ordered, Ann told Jim.

Jim glanced at his watch and noticing that it was getting late in the afternoon wondered where Don and Brenda had wandered off to. He expected them to be back before now. Even if the fishing was good, the sun was too hot to be out all afternoon.

He told Ann that it was about time for David and the others to be returning from their visit from the Mullins' house. Jim hoped it was a successful trip. The Mullins had to help them with the task of moving or getting the grave moved back to where Joshua was. Ann thought to herself that here they had been all morning and early afternoon without the appearance of Rebecca. Jim was thinking the same thing. He wanted to believe that she wouldn't show up while it was just the two of them.

Ann asked Jim, "Wonder if Rebecca's spirit can leave this area and follow David to the Mullins' place?"

"I don't have any idea what a spirit can do, but I would put money on it. She hasn't shown up here today so something's up," he replied. All afternoon Jim's thoughts were on his wife now that they were alone on the boat. He fixed them a glass of tea and took it to her.

Then gave her a kiss as he handed it to her. It differently wasn't the kind of kiss that you give as a gentle peck. It was long and wanting kiss. She hadn't had one of those since this whole vacation started. Ann needed the attention of her husband more than either one of them knew at the time. She answered his kiss with a deeper more tempting reply. As they stood on the sun deck he again kissed her gently, persuading rather than forcing. His hands moved her body to his. This made his arousal obvious to her.

"Now see what you've done to me," he said against her lips. "Sure, blame me," she whispered back at him.

"Who else should I blame?" he answered. He kissed her again, harder and deeper, more urgent than before. He was attracted to her, like the first time they had met years ago . When he broke from her he didn't release her but buried his face in her neck, planting small kisses all over her neck, ears and throat . His hands moved to feel her body.

"Ann," he whispered softly. Thrilled by his desire, hungry with her need for him, she held him to her, closer until the heat and desire took total control of them both. Afterwards they lay in each other's arms and knew they were more relaxed than they were a half hour ago. Maybe more than they had been since this vacation started.

It was hard to find a free moment on board. The coves were private enough for time alone, for a quick lovemaking session. But this was great and they both cherished it. He leaned over and gave her a kiss and said that something was apparently wrong with Don and Brenda. It was now almost four and a half hours since they had left the houseboat. The sun was high in the sky and the heat was almost unbearable.

Ann told Jim that as soon as David and the others brought back the other runabout that he, John and David needed to start looking for them.

They had headed east around the shoreline, so that was the way to start looking for them. "Jim, maybe something's happened to our boat," she said.

"If so they could have pulled into a cove and got out of the sun by finding a shady spot to stay under. Don't worry Honey, we will find them. After all they're smart people and Don will take care of Brenda," Jim said trying to sound encouraging.

"I know, but this whole trip has been met with unexpected events. So I'm a little edgy I guess." she replied. Ann heard the sound of a boat coming nearer to the houseboat and prayed it was Don and Brenda coming back. It wasn't but it was David and the others returning from their meeting with the Mullins family.

Jim and Ann both stood on the back of the boat hoping that they brought back good news with them, that the grave could be moved back where Rebecca wanted to be. They only had three days left of this vacation and they would have to move fast, if they were to help Rebecca Jean.

Brenda could feel the tension building in her but knew that it wouldn't do any good for her to let Don know how she was feeling. He had moved the boat over to the shore and helped Brenda out of the boat so she was on the bank. Breaking the silence between them, he said that they would wait there for David or Jim to come looking for them.

To keep her mind off their problems he had her gather wood so if they were still here at dark they could have a fire. This would make it easier to find them. But he knew that sometimes the night air was chilly, surprisingly so, since the day was scorching. He prayed that this would not be the case, after all it was just late afternoon and there was plenty of daylight left.

He took a large beach towel and laid it out on the ground for them to sit on. It was underneath a tall oak tree. As they waited for help they decided to walk around the shoreline and see what they could discover that might be interesting. They had made a large pile of wood ready for burning at dark if this is where they would be.

Don was worried about Brenda but tried to keep things on a cheerful note. Without him knowing it she was doing the same. Don wondered if maybe the boat would start if he tried it one more time. As Brenda walked around exploring, he decided to get into the runabout and see if the engine would start now that it had sat for an hour or so. He had left his watch on the houseboat so he didn't have any idea what time it was.

Brenda saw a path to the right of her and decided to follow it for a bit to see where it led. For some reason it was as if she had seen the area before but she couldn't have, she told herself. As she walked along the path she felt there was someone with her. She stopped and looked back but no one was there, then all of a sudden, she heard the sound of footsteps, it went right past her and on up the path.

There were leaves that were dried on the path and as the footsteps got closer she could see the leaves being pressed down. Maybe she was being a little jumpy and started up the path again.

Then she heard the noise again behind her. She stopped. The noise stopped, too. Someone was following her, was with her right now. Her heart was thumping, and she wondered why this was happening. Maybe it was Rebecca, she thought. No, it had to be her imagination getting the best of her. She decided to return to where Don was, not to go any farther up the path.

As she rounded the bend she saw Don checking the runabout. Hurrying to him she asked him if it was running now. "No, not yet." he said as he looked in her direction. "You look strange honey, what wrong?"

"Oh, I'm probably imagining things," she said. "Pure imagination. I don't know why I'm going on like this."

"What do you mean?" he demanded.

"I was following a path over there by the big trees that led back in the woods some and before I knew it I felt someone was with me, but not visible, know what I mean?" she answered.

"Why don't I take a walk with you? You show me the path and lets go see where it leads, Okay?" Don told her.

Off they went back up the path. "Do you think we will miss the others when they come looking for us? Maybe we should go back?" Brenda asked.

"Stop with all the questions, Honey, if they find the boat they will stay there until we get back so don't worry." Don said. After taking the path for about twenty minutes they came to a clearing and there before them was a pool of water with a tree that was extending across the other end of it. Suddenly, they were both aware of where they were.

"Oh my God," Don said. "We are in the cove where Joshua is. That's why everything looked so familiar to you, Brenda." His heart was racing now. He was certain that his dream, wasn't a dream at all. That Joshua was on board the runabout while they were asleep. He could not let his fear get the best of him now.

Tears had begun to form in Brenda's eyes. She wanted to control them but it was too late, they rolled down her cheek. Don put his arms around her to reassure her everything was going to be okay. He knew they needed to get the hell out of that cove now, right now!

"Lets go back the short cut we took last time we were here," he said as they started back to the runabout. As they came closer to the shoreline where the boat was pulled up on the bank, with strange suddenness the wind picked up. Don took and held Brenda's hand while they walked as fast as they could down the path, but the wind almost blew them down.

They reached the water's edge and the wind stopped as suddenly as it had begun. The runabout was afloat in the center of the cove. For a space of five seconds Don's heart seemed to stop beating as he looked at the boat. He knew he had to go in the water and retrieve the runabout but the terror of Joshua paralyzed him.

The runabout had been set adrift by Joshua, that was for sure. The spirit wanted him in the water. Don had no choice but to go in after the boat. The terror he felt was now becoming something else altogether. Like an instinct of self-preservation, he dove into the water and swam wildly with both arms going as fast as they could carry him to the boat.

He climbed aboard and sat there for a moment resting his body. He was shaking all over, weak in the legs and arms. He had never been so shaky. Brenda stood watching him, praying that he would be all right.

Don glanced over in her direction and said he would paddle it back to her. As he looked in her direction again he was shocked with terror. There stood Joshua next to Brenda waving his hand. He was as vivid as if he were alive. Don knew Brenda wasn't aware of Joshua standing next to her. He found the paddle and started to paddle as fast as he could back in her direction but as hard as he paddled he didn't go anywhere.

This can't be happening, Don thought. He was using the paddles in the right manner to get him back into shore but that isn't what happened at all. He was moving away from

Brenda and the shoreline back to the entrance of the cove. He paddled harder but to no avail. He still moved in the wrong direction.

Brenda called to Don to come back but he wasn't in control of the boat. Joshua was! He was moving the boat and Don in the other direction. Brenda stood frightened as never before. She knew Don was trying to reach her.

The runabout moved swiftly through the water away from Brenda and the bank where she stood. The engine wasn't running but the boat was moving fast as if it was turned on. Don sat helpless knowing Joshua was behind this. He couldn't look back at Brenda anymore for he could feel the fear for her and him. Joshua had to be stopped somehow. Brenda yelled for Don to not leave her and she was becoming panicked. Don was afraid she would try to swim to him and at that moment his thought became reality.

Brenda dove into the water and was swimming his way. He knew it was too far for her to swim. What was this ghost trying to do?

He'd had enough. His mind was on Brenda and not of what might happen to him. He jumped into the water and started back to Brenda. The water was getting cold or it seemed to be to him. His mind was whirling and his fear was great. He knew that something had to stop this powerful spirit from drowning them both. But he had no idea of what or how to accomplish this.

Brenda had stopped for a rest. She was tiring quickly and tears were streaming down her face. He could hear her crying as he got closer to her. Just as she stopped for the third time, he saw her disappear under the water.

"Oh my God! No!" he screamed, "Joshua No, we know where Rebecca is."

As he finished the word Rebecca, Brenda's head popped up to the surface of the water. He swam faster and harder to get to her. Then something was at his legs pulling him down. He fought for his life. He couldn't stay down long because of his excitement.

This was it he was going to die right here and now. He could hold his breath no longer. His lungs felt like they were going to explode. Just as he felt himself start to take in water and blackness engulfed him, someone pushed him to the surface, and not a moment too soon.

He gasp for air, knowing Joshua was the one who brought him up to the surface and was the one who pulled him down. This meant he was toying with the two of them. Don knew from the first night he saw Joshua that this was a wild, distressed and driven spirit that was hell bent on getting even with the living.

He made it to Brenda and Joshua let them swim to the bank. They collapsed on the bank where Don had laid the towel down earlier. Don's feelings had undergone a change since he knew it was because of Rebecca being moved to another area away from her family, but why would he want to kill anyone? That is what he was capable of and now had almost accomplished. *What would he do to them next?* Don thought.

Somehow he had to get Joshua to listen to him about them trying to help get Rebecca and him back together. He thought about just talking out loud in hopes that Joshua would be close to them and hear what Don was saying.

So Don started talking in the air and Brenda watched knowing this had to work or they were in very big trouble. Don talked about finding Rebecca's headstone and about the locket she gave them and that they were right this moment trying to get the Mullins family to help move Rebecca back to him, that he should help them just like his lovely wife had been helping.

Don looked over at Brenda and said. "I hope this is working or we are in for a rough time ahead." Brenda leaned over and kissed him. They sat and watched the boat move back in their direction as if someone was on board. As they watched they saw someone was driving the boat, it was Joshua. The boat came up on the bank just like Don had put it there before. As it stopped the spirit of Joshua disappeared without anything else happening.

"He brought it back to us, Don." Brenda told him. They stood up and went to get in the runabout. Don turned the key and it started right up. They headed out of the cove, but not before Don told Joshua that Rebecca would be back with him and Grace real soon. Back to the houseboat they went.

They rounded the bend and saw that David and the other runabout were headed for them. Don slowed the boat and David came along side. First words out of David's mouth were, "Where in the hell have you two been for the last five hours? We were ready to call the marine patrol to start looking for you."

"It's a long story so let's wait till we get back to the houseboat and we'll tell you about our fishing trip," replied Don. Putting the boats in high gear, they both headed back to the Stardust.

They tied up the runabouts and went to the front of the boat where the others waited impatiently. Ann went to give Brenda and Don a hug and tell them she was glad they were back. Betty went to the galley and made drinks for everyone.

Before they had a chance to talk or even take a drink of the refreshments that Betty had made, they heard a small motorboat heading into the cove. They went to meet it on the back of the houseboat. David was shocked to see that it was Mr. Mullins and a young man about twenty-five. They welcomed them aboard and went back to the front sun deck where they had more room to sit and talk.

David asked Tom on the way to the front if anything was wrong. He nodded his head that, yes, something was wrong. They all took a chair and Betty went to get Tom and the young man a drink of ice tea. Tom told them that after they left his house, he and his wife had gone into town to the Court House to talk to a couple of friends about the removal of the grave.

"I found out that they won't let us move the grave and if we try they will stop us or anyone else. We can't very well go doin' it without their approval so I knew you should be told as soon as my old legs could get me here. What do you young folks reckon on doing now that you know this?" Tom asked.

David sat still for a moment and then looked at Mr. Mullins and the young man with eyes of determination in them. Before he could speak Don jumped up and announced that the grave had to be moved because he had told Joshua they were going to help return his beloved wife to him.

The young man, named LeRoy, just looked at Don in amazement and said, "Do you talk to the dead very often?" and with that laughed at Don.

Don told them what had taken place this afternoon and they sat with concern on their face, with the exception of LeRoy. He didn't believe in ghosts, even through he had heard from others all his life that they do exist. Ghosts weren't news to these hills. People had been seeing them for ages. Tom didn't know what to make of Don's story of Joshua, so he stayed quiet.

Jim stood listening to Don with fear knocking at his heart. He hesitated asking what they were going to do or how they were going to move the grave.

Then, everyone heard desperate crying and smelled orange blossoms. They knew Rebecca was close to them. They looked around but saw nothing, no signs of her. Jim rubbed his head and looked around for an answer when Ann said to them that Rebecca was over at the table.

LeRoy and Tom saw what was a faint but very distinct figure of a woman in a long dress and beautiful hair standing in front of the table to their left weeping loudly. It was again almost unbearable to hear. Tom sat back down in his seat and looked at her. He remembered the photo of her that was taken from the library. He had never seen a ghost before in his seventy years. This was one of his own family members from the past; standing on board this boat weeping in the same dress she was put to rest in.

What these here people had been saying was true, every last word. "She was such a beauty," he said out aloud to the others. LeRoy didn't make a move or utter a sound. He was spellbound by the sight of her. He felt her sadness and noticed the scent of orange blossoms that surrounded her.

She was not someone you could dismiss from your mind and he wasn't sure he wanted to. He couldn't get over how lovely she was. He stood hat in hand reluctant to look away from her. Slowly she moved in his direction, gliding with grace to the spot where Tom sat and placed her hand on Tom's arm.

She stopped weeping and looked into the face of Tom Mullins and said one word with all the emotion of a grief-stricken wife and mother. "Joshua."

With that she disappeared before their eyes. Tom told the others, "We'll put matters right for this unhappy couple, if it's the last thing I do on this earth." He looked over at LeRoy and said "You'll help these folks here do the right thing, won't you LeRoy?"

"I don't know what I can do but anything that will help." he answered Tom.

"Good, then we need to get back to my house and get an earlier start in moving the grave."

David told Tom he would go to the Marina as soon as it opened in the morning and get the diving equipment needed for the dive. LeRoy told David that he also knew how to use the equipment and would go down with him. David told Tom to go back home and get some rest that first thing in the morning would be the right time to start and with LeRoy's help along with Betty's that he would work out a plan that would accomplish moving Rebecca.

The only trouble would be if they got caught while moving the grave. So the rest of them would have to stand guard. They must not let anyone know what they were doing. If they got caught they would be sent to jail

David thought to himself, but said out loud, "Would the removal of the headstone alone do the trick?" No one answered. "We will need lights and some digging equipment" LeRoy told David. He agreed with him and asked if maybe he and Tom could get the equipment they would need to dig. Tom said they would.

"If I go to the Marina and ask for the digging equipment and lights they will know something is up."

"Don't think a thing about it. We will take care of the things you will need," replied Tom.

LeRoy asked David, "Its probably trespassing on government property if they find out what we're doing, isn't it, and if that is it they will prosecute, won't they?"

David didn't answer for a bit. He wasn't sure what they would be charged with but trespassing would be the least of their worries. LeRoy looked a little worried but didn't say a thing except that he would take the chance.

John and Lilly hadn't said a word the whole time, not since Tom and LeRoy had come aboard. They knew the others were as worried as they were and there was no need to say so. Lilly went into the galley to fix dinner for everyone. She wasn't completely satisfied with things and was afraid that something would go wrong. It wasn't for her to put a damper on things by letting them know how she felt. Tom told them he would say good evening and head for home. LeRoy said good night, and that he would be ready first thing in the morning. He wasn't so sure he could fall asleep tonight.

After Tom and LeRoy left the houseboat the others helped Lilly get dinner on the table and as they sat down to eat no one said a word. The silence remained all through dinner.

David and the other guys went out on the back sun deck to plan out what would take place in the morning. David said that they surely could find the grave and maybe if their luck held up they wouldn't have to go very deep to find the coffin. The only part that would be a little tricky would be in pulling up the coffin and keeping other boaters from knowing something was going on.

This is where Jim and John said they would take over to insure no one knew what was happening under the water. The secrets below the water would remain there if they were successful. David said that they would tie a rope around the coffin before it was raised to hold it together. Then raise it to just below the surface of the water by tying it to the bottom of the runabout. This way they could move it through the water without being seen.

He said he would drive the runabout while Jim and John appeared to be fishing. Maybe the other people wouldn't wonder what they were doing. David told them that the second runabout would have Lilly and Brenda in it waiting for them to come up after the coffin was tied to the rope and ready for transporting. They all headed for bed early so they could get plenty of rest. It was hard for any of them to sleep.

Lilly's feeling of doom was still with her. She decided to stay up awhile and read. This would tire her and then she would go to sleep. They were all asleep in record time. Lilly sat reading, thinking all the while about what would happen in the morning. She went out on the front bow of the boat to walk around and try to calm herself down. But as the minutes went on she became more uneasy.

She sometimes felt things other people never did and this was one of the times she wished she didn't have the ability. It made her feel quite odd. After she walked around the outside of the Stardust a couple of times she knew she could go to bed and possibly sleep.

On the second time around the boat's exterior she stopped by the front bow to look at the stars up in the night sky. The stars twinkled like wonderful faceted diamonds. It was a very clear night and there was an owl in one of the trees near the houseboat that hooted at her. She smiled to herself and thought how wonderful the fresh night air was. She wondered if other people in big cities ever look up in the night sky and at the stars. They were as bright as she had ever seen before.

The night sounds were reassuring to hear and made her want to sleep, so she headed to bed. They had just three more days in this wonderful place. Even though they had the problems with the spirits of Joshua and Rebecca, they did enjoy the trip down here to this beautiful lake. If everything went well the next day or so, they would all return again.

Everyone knew that in the morning three of them would descend down to the bottom of this lake and risk their lives to put things right that went wrong years before. Rebecca and Joshua had captured their hearts and souls. They were risking their lives and maybe jail against almost impossible odds.

DAY EIGHT

It was a lovely site to see, the big red ball rising up over the mountains. The sky was beautiful with color. The sun felt great because the night was cool. There wasn't a cloud in the sky and they all hoped that rain wasn't in the forecast for the next few days. No one on board the houseboat wanted breakfast this morning. David wondered if Tom Mullins and his wife were up and he hoped LeRoy didn't forget the items they needed for the dive.

After everyone was up and having coffee, David asked John if he would ride over to the marina with him to pick up the diving equipment. John said yes and Betty told David she would like to go along, too. She wanted to get a smaller facemask. The one she had before wasn't a good fit. They untied the runabout and headed to the Marina, telling the others they would be back in a short time. The others watched as the runabout left the cove for the main part of the lake.

Lilly took her cup of coffee out on the front of the boat. As she took a seat she noticed she wasn't alone but that Rebecca was there on the bow. Just staring off in the direction of the other cove where her beloved Joshua was. Lilly didn't say a word but just watched her for a while before Ann came out to join her. Ann had not seen Rebecca but smelled the orange blossoms in the air and knew that Rebecca was near.

With a heavy sigh, Ann asked Lilly, "Do you think they will be all right down there today?"

"They will if we don't get company from the other divers." Lilly said as she once more glanced in the direction of the bow where Rebecca had been only minutes earlier.

"Brenda is getting things together for lunch. We should help her pack because we won't be back for quite some time," Ann suggested.

"Well, lets go help and see that we have enough." Lilly answered. About an hour after David had gone to the marina, Mr. Mullins and LeRoy arrived in LeRoy's small motorboat he used for fishing. They had everything they had promised to bring.

Tom took a cup of coffee and went to sit down next to Jim and Don. LeRoy was checking everything over again. Jim watched him and told Tom he thought LeRoy was maybe a little young for all this. Tom watched the boy for a while and said, "He's young but he's shore got the ability to learn quickly and I don't reckon he gets rattled under these here types of pressure. He was a navy man you know."

Jim nodded his head in agreement. Don was looking out on the lake. His eyes narrowed against the sun shining brightly across the lake in front of him. Shading his eyes against the sun, he watched as a boat moved fast in his direction. It was David, he knew. He could hear the engine and knew it was the runabout.

David brought the runabout up along side the Stardust. Jim and LeRoy helped to tie up the boat. Betty was glad to see that Tom and LeRoy were already there. David told the ladies to get ready to leave. Him and the other men loaded the equipment for diving, and the auger, the vac, shovels and lights that Tom had picked up last night. They headed for the area off Diver's Island where they knew the headstone laid in the deep waters of Eagle's Lake.

The big job was now underway. David told them what he wanted them to do. He studied LeRoy for a moment then asked the young man if he had been down over a hundred feet before.

"I don't think I have been that deep in the past four years or so," he replied. David knew he sounded a little nervous but he didn't look afraid. Which made David and Betty feel better. Tom looked over at LeRoy and said, "Nothing to it, son, God be with you."

Betty, LeRoy and David suited up. "Now, you do remember the best way to leave the boat don't you," David asked LeRoy with a laugh to break the silence. "Backward, over the side of the boat," LeRoy answered while lowering his goggles, he put his mouthpiece in place, sat on the edge of the boat and flipped over into the water. One by one they left the side of the runabout and in seconds were gone from sight.

The second boat was a decoy for them. It was the girls who were to watch and look like they were sun bathing while they let the guys in the other boat fish. Girls in one, guys in the other. Jim told John and Don to get the fishing gear and start to fish. They needed to have fish on board if the wildlife patrol checked them. It really had to seem that they were only fishing and nothing else.

During the descent the three switched on the underwater lights. They had reached the bottom of the lake a few seconds later. David and Betty started looking for the place where they had seen the headstone of Rebecca.

When they found it, David started to show Betty and LeRoy how to place the ropes around the stone so the others on board the runabout could pull it up without any trouble of it coming lose and dropping. It would take the three on board the runabout to lift it out of the water. They had blankets on the boat to cover the headstone.

The whole idea was to get the coffin on ropes and pull it up under the boat and move it slowly in the direction of the cove where it was to be placed back down on the lake's bottom. It took quite awhile for them to get the stone tied securely and signal the others on top to start pulling it up. They had hooked the portable lights up right in the place where the headstone was and David started to use the auger to dig slowly downward.

They knew the coffin was made of just hard pinewood. It was about six to seven feet down and they had to go slow so the water would be clear enough to see in. After all, the sediment would be stirred up due to the auger and the portable vac. Meanwhile the guys were pulling up the headstone very, very slowly.

No other boats had come within five hundred feet of them so far today. Things were working out great. It was hard going for the divers to remove the lake's bottom and hope at the same time that it was the right spot to dig. Heavy rocks had to be moved at times and it took all three to accomplish this task.

It was taking them longer to dig and clear the hole than they had imagined. Betty kept the lights focused on the spot but had a terrible, sinking feeling gripping at her stomach. Would they have enough time to finish the job before they were due to return the houseboat? She knew within her heart that they had to stay till the job was finished.

They glimpsed a shadow pass over them and it caught their attention. As they looked up they could see another boat had joined the two runabouts up on top. David motioned for Betty and LeRoy to stop what they were doing. She cut off the light and LeRoy stopped the vac so the dirt could settle. They watched for the boat to move off or to get a sign from the others on board the runabouts. LeRoy took the chalkboard he had brought with him and wrote a message to David that maybe he should go to the surface if the boat stayed much longer. David shook his head no, took the board and wrote back, "They can handle anything that may come up, so don't worry."

They watched, but David couldn't tolerate the delay. His impatience was showing. LeRoy swam over to the spot where they had put the tools and came back with a small shovel and handed it to David. David nodded his head in agreement and began to dig with the small shovel while LeRoy and Betty kept an eye on the surface of the water.

Meanwhile the others had a visitor with them from the Wildlife Patrol and he was staying with them for awhile. Lieutenant Morgan was his name. He had been around the lake about a half dozen times this morning and always noticed them being in this one area and wondered if something was the matter or if the fishing was that good where they were.

He had also asked about the fire extinguishers and fishing permits, plus if there were life jackets in the boat for everyone. Lilly found he was a nice man just checking them out to see if he could be of assistance.

He wasn't in any hurry to leave them and this alone worried Lilly because of the things going on the bottom of the lake. She hoped they had seen that there was another boat up top, and that they wouldn't need the other air tanks before this man left the area.

They had taken a small air compressor that ran off batteries to use with the water vac. Her thoughts were interrupted by hearing John tell the officer that this lake was wonderful with it's clear turquoise water and great fishing. Jim added that he liked the cleanliness of the water and the private coves.

The officer said he had grown up there and loved the area and lake so much that he decided to stay here and live instead of going to the big cities. He liked the quiet country life.

"Well, folks, I had better get going and let you get back to catching the big ones," he said jokingly then added, "Maybe I'll see you around later," which was not what Jim wanted to hear.

Betty watched as the boat left and David started digging with the auger again. The water was becoming quite dirty and muddy from the auger and the vac. They would have to wait for the water to clear before going on.

So at this time they headed up top to exchange air tanks and grab something to eat and drink. Jim told David that the Wildlife

Patrol was there but not to worry he was just making sure they were okay.

Jim asked, "How are you coming with things down there?"

LeRoy answered first with, "Very slow, we are maybe three feet down."

"That's all?" John asked, startled.

"We came up while we waited for the dirt to settle down. It was getting too thick to see. The underwater flashlights didn't help at all with the mud getting thick in the water."

"It was dark, total darkness almost," Betty told them.

Ann asked Betty if that was hard to take, being down there with just the flashlights to see with and not being able to see at least three or four feet in any direction. She informed them all that when David and she got their certifications they had to pass a test, which eighty percent of the class failed. It was to find out how one would react or handle themselves in total darkness underwater.

"Oh yeah?" Ann asked while looking concerned. "Why did some fail?"

"They would almost go crazy from claustrophobia."

"Really," replied Ann.

"When you consider being down there in total darkness, in cold water and the silence, only hearing your own heart pounding, it can really get to you. You start imagining all kind of strange things. Hey, its beautiful down there, don't get me wrong. We just stirred up the water a little too much. The water here would be easy to see in as long as we didn't stir it up from the digging," Betty told them. "We will use the shovels if we have to. That will cut down on the noise and mud," David said, "Lets hit the water crew and don't waste anymore time than we have to. It's going to be a long haul anyway, I think, because we are moving too slow for my liking."

They placed their masks and air tanks back on and descended back down to the grave. The water had cleared altogether by now and they could see where they had left off. David motioned to LeRoy to use the shovels for the time being. They had dug about four feet down and he wanted them to go quickly, but not fast enough to hit the coffin by accident. The wooden coffin was old and if the shovel hit it hard enough, it may damage the wood and they may not be able to tie ropes and lift it up under the boat.

It was getting later in the afternoon when Jim decided to let the girls go to the houseboat for a break and some more drinking water. He knew that they would be there for quite sometime.

Ann said they would hurry back as soon as they could get the things they needed. Jim asked Tom if he would like to go with them and get some rest. He was looking tired and for a man seventy years old, he didn't need to be out here in this unbearable heat. He agreed that he did need to rest and he could do that on board the houseboat. John even inquired as to taking him home for the day.

"No way," he replied with certainty in his voice. "This old man ain't going home till the job's done, son, you hear!"

Off they headed to the Stardust. They fixed Tom a bed on the sofa and told him to just relax and take a nap.

The water remained clearer with them using the shovels but it was hard on them. They were getting exhausted and Betty feared David was pushing himself too hard. This might cloud his judgment and he needed to be alert. She didn't know whether or not to try to get him to stop for a time and let her and LeRoy work for a while. This way, he could hold the flashlights and see how things were progressing.

Betty also noticed that it was getting dark and that the others on the surface might need to take a break and go to the houseboat.

Just as she was ready to motion to David and LeRoy, something caught her eye just over David's left shoulder. It was a beam of light, vague, dim, barely discernible inside this muck that was being stirred up. Maybe it was some refraction from the lights they were using.

She was getting herself completely spooked. It was coming in their direction and moving with some speed. As she watched, it moved out of their directional path a ways. She wished the water were clearer like it was normally. She thought that maybe anything could exist down here, maybe there were other ghosts, not just their Rebecca.

Underwater the rules are different. Anything goes. The light by this time had moved totally off in the other direction. David and LeRoy worked at a steady pace. Betty again saw the light floating back, then suddenly coming straight at them.

Oh, no, she thought, *its another diver.* She was sure of it. What was she to do at this point. She tapped David on the arm and pointed over his shoulder. He looked inquiringly at her, and then turned to look at what she was showing him and noticed that they weren't alone anymore. There, approaching them were two other divers. David took the chalkboard and wrote, "We are studying the area and hope you will leave us to our work."

They came up next to LeRoy and looked down at the area where David had been using the shovel and held out their arms as if to say, "What are you doing?"

David showed them the chalkboard and they nodded their heads that they would leave. They hadn't seen anything that would make them believe something unlawful was going on. They swam in the direction of the east side of Divers Island. David had a feeling that they would cause trouble anyway and motioned to Betty and LeRoy that they all should go up for the time being.

Betty turned off the lights and LeRoy placed the shovels on top the grave area. Then they stared up together to the runabout. As they reached the surface David noticed how dark it had become since they were here a couple hours ago. If they were going to work through the night he hoped it would not be a clear night. His hope had become reality.

The thing about needing a cloudy night to do what you need to do, what ever that may be, means you must accept the clouds with all their implications, which in this case could be a storm. Jim had been sitting there with Don and John, bored, sleepy and a little apprehensive about whether they were okay down there. He was so glad to have them aboard and on their way back to the girls and the Stardust, he clapped his hands as they climbed onto the runabout.

As they arrived back at the houseboat, before going inside, John felt a drop of water hit his hand as he tied the runabout up to the houseboat. He wiped it off and thought that it came from the rope, but then another drop, and another and he knew it was starting to rain. "Hey, you guys can't go back out in this kind of weather," he said.

Betty turned and looked up at the sky. It was completely overcast, no stars were showing at all.

"We need this kind of weather to not draw attention to us and you guys in the boat. We must go back down as soon as we can. Grab something to eat and rest for a while. We need all the time we can get when the lake isn't busy," David said feeling like he could easily be talked into stopping and waiting till morning. He felt like his arms weren't a part of him anymore. He hadn't worked this hard in months. He said to LeRoy, "You were a big help down there today and I hope you aren't too tired to go back down with us a little later."

"I'll be fine after I get some hot food in me. You know that the next part will be tricky, if it is raining. I just hope there won't be a storm, just a slight rain shower." LeRoy replied.

Tom had been awake for sometime now and Betty asked him if Mrs. Mullins would be all right with him not calling her to let her know he was okay. He said that she knew all right that these here things could take a long time and she agreed that this was necessary. "My gal's a tough cookie." he said.

After about an hour and a half they were ready to head back to the grave. Jim wasn't really looking forward to going back out there in this kind of weather. The rain was coming down quite steadily, but there weren't any signs of a storm approaching, yet.

They floated over to the spot and Betty, David and LeRoy put their gear back on. They had left the wetsuits on, and now entering the water, they felt the coldness even through the suits. Jim had put the top up on the runabout but still he wondered if it would give them enough protection from the rain. When it rained sometimes it poured like a water faucet, filling the boat floor with water.

He then remembered the runabout had a pump. He could just flip the button and the pump would get rid of the water. He had, like

John and Don, put on extra clothes and wore a waterproof jacket. Still the wind was chilly to them.

It was so dark that they had trouble seeing what was going on in the boat. Don brought along his big flashlight and turned it on till the others left the boat for the bottom of the lake.

They descended to the bottom and felt the loneliness there that had become more intense. They could barely see anything at all in front of them. Betty held the lights as close to them as she could without being in the way. They used the shovels and were flinging mud everywhere.

David stopped to measure the distance of feet they had reached by this time. It was five to six feet down. He signaled the others and showed them so that LeRoy would take his time and go slower.

Betty was feeling so anxious about this that she was not paying much attention to anything else except for David and LeRoy. She knew that at any minute they would hit the coffin. They had to. It was the only thing on her mind at this time.

Thud, went the sound that all three heard at the same time. David's shovel had hit something solid. Something wood. As they looked at each other they knew this was the grave of Rebecca Jean Collins. It had to be. Their pleasure made them forget the others on top, and then Betty motioned to them she was going up to tell Jim and the rest that the coffin was found.

Meanwhile David and LeRoy inched theirs shovels around the sides of the coffin to loosen the mud and remove more and more mud from the top of the coffin. They cleared the sides almost all the way around the casket and now they could ease the ropes beneath it and pull it up out of it's cradle.

As they tied the ropes off, LeRoy went to get the main rope that would keep it in place under the runabout. David thought, if they could somehow use their air tanks to help lift the coffin it would make it easy for them to get it to the surface. When LeRoy returned with the rope they found it was quite easy to pull the casket up because the wood was still buoyant and had a tendency to float.

Slowly and reluctantly, after so many years in this spot the coffin with Rebecca started to lift out of it's cradle. Once it was accessible to them they finished tying the ropes that would carry it to the new resting place, with Joshua.

They needed new air tanks and so they decided to go up and rest before securing it to the runabout for it's journey back to the cove where it should have been left. David knew that what was needed was a winch and they didn't have one, but maybe they could rig something up that would work just the same. This would make it easier for rasing the coffin and attaching it underneath the runabout. Betty made it to the surface in record time.

As she hit the surface she noticed that there was someone else there with Jim and the guys. Another boat. She had been so excited about the coffin that she hadn't paid attention to the surface. After all it was night, rainy and who would be out in this kind of weather anyway.

There in the boat was Lt. Morgan and the two divers that she had seen earlier in the day. "Well gentlemen help the young lady aboard. What is a woman like yourself doing scuba diving this time of night?" he asked her. She went weak all over as they helped her on board. He didn't give her a chance to answer his question before he ask the two others if she was one of the people they had seen earlier down at the bottom digging a hole. They answered that she was.

Lt. Morgan studied her for a moment and noticed that she was kind of anxious about something and he didn't believe it was because of him and the other men. There was something else he saw in her manner. "Well, are we keeping you from anything?" he said looking at her with deep interest. "No, Lt. Morgan I just like to dive at night," she feebly said. Oh God, what was going to happen to us now she thought. Hearing a noise at the end of the boat near the ladder they looked to see what it was. David and LeRoy had topped the surface of the water near the ladder before they saw the others on board the boat.

"What do we have here?" the Lieutenant said with great pleasure. LeRoy and David climbed on board the runabout and took off their air tanks and goggles. "What the hell are you folks doing out in the rain diving in this water this time of night, tell me!" he demanded.

They didn't answer right away and David wasn't sure what to say when he did answer. "You all are up to your eyeballs in something and you are going to talk to me or I'm going to take you in. These two men saw you earlier on the bottom digging a hole like you were burying something. What was it you were getting rid of anyway?"

LeRoy knew the Lieutenant and his family. He was from these parts and might understand if they leveled with him. David said he was doing a study on the ground and soil samples down there. That he studied rocks and the earth's crust.

"Bull shit", said the Lieutenant. "You will have to follow me into the Marina. Don't try to get away. I'm taking you in to the office to see if maybe we can find out what is happening down there come morning." Helpless, David stared at Betty. She looked so small and defeated. Jim was uneasy with the situation. He knew that if they waited till morning everything would be found out and they would be charged with, WOW, a lot of things.

LeRoy told the Lieutenant to wait a moment that he would like to talk to David. He nodded okay. LeRoy told David and the rest of the crew, "We must take our chances and tell him what we are doing and why. Tom is a relative and that makes a difference. This lieutenant is from these parts and knows of ghosts and spirits. He may listen to me."

David's first reaction was to say no. The look on LeRoy's face made him reconsider. "I guess it's all right," David said. LeRoy confided that he would tell him the whole story and he did, but the Lieutenant laughed at them. "Let's get a move on." he said.

But just as he started to turn the engine on the breeze picked up and gently messed his salt-and-pepper hair. The air was humid but there was something else in it also. The breeze swirled around Lt. Morgan only and then a pale white figure took form in front of his eyes. It was Rebecca and she stood weeping softly. There was a shadow of fear in his eyes. He had witnessed other happenings with spirits, but this was one of a kind.

She was beautiful, but very sad. LeRoy told him they must move her back with her family or no one would leave this spot and he could assure him of that. There was no one around but you could see the lights of red and green flicker off in the distance. It was other fishing boats. He knew he must make a decision and make it soon.

Rebecca just stayed there in the air floating about two feet off the deck. "Okay, okay dammit," he announced. "Do what you must and be out of here by tomorrow night because I won't be the one on duty then."

The two other divers hadn't taken their eyes off Rebecca and never moved an inch. Lt. Morgan started his boat and told the men to sit still; he would drop them at their boat on the way to the marina. He reassured LeRoy and the others that the two men wouldn't cause them any more trouble. He yelled, "Good luck." as he moved away.

All they wanted to do at this point was to get back to the coffin, get it moved and get themselves out of this whole thing.

They put on their goggles and air tanks and over they went into the water and down to Rebecca's coffin. David had lowered the main rope from the runabout and now started to fix it around the coffin. LeRoy helped and within minutes they were finished tying it securely.

They pulled on the rope a couple of times to let Jim and Don know to start to pull the rope slowly up till it was directly under and touching the bottom of the runabout. This way they could move very slowly through the water to the other cove.

It was beginning to get light and the sun would be rising soon. They must move it while it's early. It was just light enough to see where they were going and that's what they wanted. This way they wouldn't be seen by anyone.

Betty and David picked up the equipment and headed for the surface. LeRoy got the shovels and moved upward to the surface right behind David and Betty. He dropped the one shovel and had to go back down after it. What he didn't know was exactly how long they had been down and how much air was left in his tank. He gave it a quick thought and went on down after the shovel.

After retrieving it, he headed back up to the surface. He wondered if he would make the surface because he knew the air had to be low. David hit the surface and yelled for Jim to throw him a new air tank. Jim grabbed the new one and tossed it to David. He headed back down to LeRoy. As David reached him, about twenty feet down LeRoy was out of air. So was David and they had to share the new tank. Everyone was watching for them to rise to the top of the water.

Jim told David that they had the coffin tied up tight to the bottom of the boat, that it wasn't going anywhere. John poured them a cup of the steaming hot coffee Lilly had made for them. They relaxed for about twenty minutes and Don heard the sound of a motor coming their way. He hoped that it wasn't the Lieutenant from the Wildlife Patrol.

As the sound got closer to them he saw it was the other runabout with the girls and Tom. Lilly had woke up early and knew that they should come out to see if everything was okay. She said she had a bad dream and wanted to make sure they were all right. She had tried to go back to sleep but was wide-awake. By this time the rain had stopped.

DAY 9

They checked the ropes underneath the runabout before heading to the homeport where the coffin would come to rest. Their ordeal would soon be over and so would the ordeal for Joshua and Rebecca... years of unrest, of not ending their stay on this earth. Soon they could be at rest for all time, together finally, the way they should have been long ago.

Slowly the runabout moved in the direction of the cove with the other boat following. David and Tom talked about how they were going to put the coffin in the grave. How they would bury it. David said he and LeRoy would go down and take a look at the bottom. They knew that there wasn't anyway in hell they could dig a grave and place the coffin in it. That was out of the question.

When they moved into the cove, David and LeRoy took their air tanks and descended into the water to find where they should place the coffin. As they reached the bottom they were surprised to see the vision of Joshua. Before they went any further, they pointed up to the coffin and Joshua nodded his head and floated over to the coffin.

Rebecca's spirit joined his and they embraced each other. Joshua and Rebecca were joined by the most beautiful little girl they had ever seen. They took each other by the hand and rose to the surface. David knew that things were right for them now. They rose to the front bows of the runabouts and all of the crew on board the two boats saw them hand in hand. Rebecca wasn't weeping anymore.

Lilly even spoke to them and told them that the crew was happy that things were made right. But little did she know that David and LeRoy couldn't find a place to put the coffin and cover it to make it safe. David had a bad cramp in his leg and had to stop for a while.

LeRoy hadn't noticed that David wasn't with him and continued on looking for somewhere it could be buried. David was in pain by this time and the cramp was so bad it caused him to have trouble breathing. He had also picked up the tank that he had when they came up with the equipment. He had no air left in the tank. He couldn't move his leg because of the pain. He had taken one big breath of air before taking off the tank and opening the value so it could be used to help take him to the top of the water. He needed help and fast.

He was letting out the air slowly and trying to make it to the top. He was out of air and his lungs felt like they were going to burst. He didn't think he would make it. He knew that he was blacking out. Just as he thought he was dying he felt someone pushing him to the surface. He knew that it had to be LeRoy. But as he hit the surface he saw this pale white figure beside him and he knew it was Rebecca who had helped him reach the surface.

Betty and the others helped David aboard the runabout and took care of him. They knew LeRoy had to be all right because the spirits were there to see to it. LeRoy had come to an area where there was a trench about the size of three feet by six feet and he knew this would be perfect for Rebecca's coffin and they could cover it with dirt and stones. It was a great spot.

He turned around to tell David and noticed that he wasn't anywhere around. Had something happened to him? Back he went to the place where he had last seen David. Nothing was there so he headed for the surface. David was feeling better now that he was back on board the runabout.

"I thought I was a goner," David said. "They saved my life, you know." LeRoy came up and saw that David was on board and ask what happened. Ann told him.

"Well, I have the spot to place the coffin in and it won't take long. It's about ten feet from the shoreline over there near the trees. Don looked at the area where LeRoy was talking about and remembered the day he and Brenda had ended up here. They had almost drowned by the hand of Joshua.

The trees where he was pointing was where they had pulled into and rested that day. "How deep is the water there ?" Don asked LeRoy. "I'm not sure, but for a guess, I would say about fifty to sixty feet down." There was a trench along the bottom running out about fifteen feet to the center almost. "It's deep enough for us to place the coffin and cover it nicely," LeRoy announced with excitement.

David had rested long enough and was ready to help finish the job. He put his goggles and air tank on and over the end of the runabout he went, with LeRoy right behind him. Jim had a headache and wanted to get some sleep real soon but like the others the excitement of a job almost finished was something he didn't want to miss.

There was Brenda who was still terrified that something would still go wrong or that someone would catch them. She couldn't wait for them to be back at the houseboat with nothing to do but relax. She didn't want to see anymore ghosts for the rest of her life. This vacation had been enough for a lifetime.

The Lieutenant may decide to come back and arrest all of them. She was glad that it had only taken the one-day and night. Lilly was glad that the spirits hadn't hurt her friends. She like the others, knew that they had the power to do so if they really wanted to. You just don't mess around with spirits from another world who are locked into this world because of circumstances beyond their control.

David and LeRoy worked to get the spot ready for the coffin to be lowered into the trench. The hard job would be to cover it so it would never be found or disturbed again. They were ready in about an hour and LeRoy came up to let the others know that they were going to lower the coffin slowly into the trench now.

As he told the others what to do to help, Lilly noticed his even breathing and relaxed face suggested that things were going well down there in the resting place of the Collins family. She wondered how many other poor souls where left to this world because of similar circumstances like this one. There had to be more souls earthbound underwater like this. Maybe in larger lakes and no one knew why there were spirits in those places.

God, was she glad to have been a part of this whole thing even though it could have been bad for the others if they hadn't worked together so well.

They were lowering the coffin into the trench now and everyone was watching intensely. Hoping that nothing would go wrong at this late date. When the coffin was placed in the trench LeRoy started to place large rocks around the coffin to hold it in place. David carried rocks and placed them on top of the coffin. The flexible shaft was lowered to the grave site so that cement could be poured over and around the coffin to seal Rebecca's resting place forever.

They were proud of themselves. Then they headed up to the others with a feeling of satisfaction.

Before reaching the top they stopped and; looked back one more time. There in the beautiful clear water were Rebecca and Joshua, hand in hand, looking back at them. In an instant the images disappeared leaving them with a wonderful feeling.

No one could ever describe the feeling. They loaded all the equipment in to the runabouts and headed for the Stardust. They had only half a day left and they wanted to really enjoy the wonderful waters of Eagles Lake. As they headed out of the cove none of them looked back.

They concentrated the rest of their time at the lake on enjoying it and as they headed to the marina to return the boat and start for home, back to the city life for another year, they saw what appeared to be a faint white mist following them. Lilly got chills and wondered…

No, she thought to herself, *everything really is okay*. And they didn't give it another thought as they returned the boat and headed home.

They didn't notice but the mist was with them all the way. When they reached Ohio they went their separate ways and each wondered if they would ever see another ghost. The experience they shared would never be forgotten, yet they weren't anxious to talk about it even among themselves.

The next January, they all got together again for the annual planning of the annual vacation.

Betty asked the group, "How can we top last year's excitement?"

Jim answered with "Who wants to sail a boat through the Bermuda Triangle? I understand it can be an exciting experience!"

Sheila Terry writes as Samantha Moss.
She lives in Missouri.